'I can wait a little longer,' Alex promised.

'As long as we are together, learning things about each other.' He slid his fingers along her arm. 'Touching—like this!' He leant towards her. 'Kissing—like this!'

He's a practised seducer, Leonie reminded herself, but then his lips closed on hers and she felt the burning flame of his desire.

She pulled away from him, knowing she had to stand up to his mastery, to make her own terms in this 'relationship', so that she could survive the experience unscathed—so she could protect her peace of mind and her relationship with her children. But how?

Having pursued many careers—from school-teaching to pig farming—with varying degrees of success and plenty of enjoyment, **Meredith Webber** seized on the arrival of a computer in her house as an excuse to turn to what had always been a secret urge—writing. As she had more doctors and nurses in the family than any other professional people, the medical romance seemed the way to go! Meredith lives on the Gold Coast of Queensland, with her husband and teenage son.

Recent titles by the same author:

WINGS OF DEVOTION
WINGS OF SPIRIT
WINGS OF CARE
WINGS OF PASSION
WINGS OF DUTY
COURTING DR GROVES

WINGS OF LOVE

BY

MEREDITH WEBBER

MILLS & BOON®

All the characters in this book have no existence outside the imagination of the author, and have no relation whatsoever to anyone bearing the same name or names. They are not even distantly inspired by any individual known or unknown to the author, and all the incidents are pure invention.

First published in Great Britain 1997
Harlequin Mills & Boon Limited,
Eton House, 18-24 Paradise Road, Richmond, Surrey TW9 1SR

ISBN 0 263 15440 8

Set in Times 10 on 12 pt. by
Rowland Phototypesetting Limited
Bury St Edmunds, Suffolk

15-9708-45920-D

Printed and bound in Great Britain
by Mackays of Chatham PLC, Chatham

CHAPTER ONE

As Leonie swung into the car park she glimpsed the man, sitting on the front steps of the old house that housed the office of the Rainbow Bay Base of the Royal Flying Doctor Service. Her heart bumped unevenly, but she knew it couldn't be Alex. Hadn't she received yellow roses from him only yesterday?

She stopped the car and stared out through the windscreen at the tropical vegetation, running rampant in the garden. Alex Solano, doctor turned scientist turned successful drug manufacturer—born in the north of Italy, now living in Switzerland—father of Carlos! And somewhere in his career he'd worked in Australia for a time because he was qualified to practise here. That summarised all she *knew* of Alex—but what of her feelings?

Hopes and fears jostled for brain space. She should never have allowed herself to dream, not with the children still dependent on her.

'Do you sit there for a specified time in silent communion with the garden?'

Sweat broke out on the palms of her hands, making them slip on the leather steering-wheel cover. She turned her head towards the window and saw the man she shouldn't dream about. In the flesh! Alive and solid! And so very, very handsome!

'Alex?' she murmured, unable to accept the reality of him.

Eyes so dark they were almost black smiled down at her, and the sun struck the silver in the thick dark thatch of his hair, but it wasn't until he reached through the open window and touched her on her arm that she knew he wasn't an illusion.

'It is this weekend, isn't it?' he asked, his slight accent turning the simple words into a melody. 'The Picnic Races?'

Her gaze slid up to scan his face, fitting the features to her memories: tanned skin, stretched smooth and tight across a strong profile, dark eyebrows framing those warm, commanding eyes, and lips full and sensuous—lips that had tormented her dreams for months!

'But you rang me from Switzerland last week,' she dithered while he opened the car door for her and reached out a hand to help her stand. 'You said nothing. . .'

His fingers were cool, with a tensile strength beneath the softness. In one smooth motion he drew her to her feet and trapped her loosely against his body. The dark gaze flicked across her face, as if checking her features.

'I had already told you I would try to be back for these Picnic Races I had heard so much about. Back for them—and for something else, Leonie.'

The way he said her name made her blood run faster, thundering through her veins at breakneck speed.

'I can't. . . It won't. . . The children. . .'

The confused trickle of half-sentences were cut off by his lips, descending on hers with a purposeful intensity. And her own responded, meeting his demands with a matching hunger so that all thoughts were dissolved and there was only feeling.

'It has to be something in the water at this place,' a

cheerful voice remarked, and Leonie broke away from Alex and turned, her face flaming with heat, to see Kelly Jackson emerging from her car.

As Kelly leant over into the back seat to pull some file cases out Leonie glanced back at Alex, shock making her bones shake.

'I didn't hear a car drive in!'

He grinned at her, leant forward and kissed her gently on the forehead.

'Nor did I,' he told her, then he straightened up and, with one arm firmly around her waist, he turned her towards the new arrival.

Leonie knew she shouldn't accept such an overt signal of attraction—of possession—but his arm made her feel warm and comfortable, yet excited at the same time.

She reminded herself that she was a grown woman with responsibilities, and stepped away reluctantly. Maybe she could feel warm and comfortable and excited some other time, but in the car park outside work it wasn't an option.

'This is Kelly Jackson, a locum taking Peter's place while he and Katie are away.'

Having performed the introductions, Leonie watched Kelly reach out one hand in welcome and realised how beautiful the younger woman was. She glanced at Alex. Would he notice?

Once again shock jolted through her. Was this jealousy? She barely knew the man yet here she was, showing all the insecurities of adolescence!

Kelly explained that she would be staying on in Rainbow Bay and flashed the sapphire ring Jack had slipped on her finger only last week.

'So, I must wish you all the best for your future.

And Jack also. He is a lucky man, is he not?'

He turned to Leonie for confirmation, and she hid her uncertainty with a bright smile. Until she saw the message in his eyes—a message that caught at the breath in her throat and stopped the automatic movements of her lungs.

Something was said about Jack and the staff meeting, but Leonie was too busy breathing to make sense of the words. Alex took the cases Kelly was holding and then, with the slightest of pressures on her shoulder, urged Leonie towards the building.

Kelly went ahead and unlocked the back door. She led the way through to the main office and waved towards her desk.

'Just drop the files there,' she told Alex. 'I'll turn on the urn so we can start the day with coffee.'

As Alex moved towards the desk she glanced at Leonie, her lovely eyes dancing with delight.

'The yellow roses?' she asked lightly.

Leonie nodded hesitantly. She could feel the heat zooming back into her cheeks, and knew she was exhibiting all the symptoms of a teenager in the throes of first love.

'I'll be in my office if you need me,' she gabbled, and fled to that small refuge. The sign on the door read BASE MANAGER—it showed she was mature! Responsible!

But the scent of the roses permeated the air and filled her senses with its languorous sweetness so when Alex entered behind her she turned into his arms and let him hold her for a moment until the world steadied.

'You *are* going to the Picnic Races?' he asked, after she'd broken away from the temptation of his clasp and walked around her desk to drop into her chair. He sat down opposite her and leaned back, totally relaxed in this alien environment.

'I am!' she assured him, then added warningly, 'but, although I'm officially on holidays from this evening, I'll be representing the Service while I'm out at Talgoola.'

His crooked smile teased at her nerve endings.

'Isn't there an English expression about all work and no play?'

I should stop this undercurrent of love play right now, she told herself. Tell him how pointless it is—how impossible a relationship between us would be.

But she'd accepted his roses! Lived for his late-night phone calls—using them as a basis for impossible dreams!

'It's a weekend of madness!' she pointed out, unable to imagine this suave, sophisticated man in such a setting. Unable to imagine the effect his being there would have on her confused mind and unreliable body.

'I am staying a month, Leonie: we will have time,' he said quietly, and she wondered if he'd felt the panic rustling through her like a hidden breeze, stirring the dead pages of the past and her placid vision of an unexciting future.

She looked into his eyes and glimpsed steel beneath the softness, but the other things those eyes were saying made her forget her forebodings as her body responded with a pulsing urgency and her mouth grew dry.

'I've so much work to do before I leave for Talgoola in the morning. . .' she muttered at him, turning away from his dynamic appeal and waving a feeble hand towards the piles of paperwork littering her desk.

He grasped the moving hand and squeezed her fingers with a reassuring pressure.

'You want me out of your way,' he murmured smoothly. 'You are right, I will go! I will wait for Jack in the radio room.'

He pushed back his chair and stood up so that she had to peer up at him as she echoed, 'Jack?'

'I phoned him last evening. We have an appointment at nine.'

A final tightening of fingers and he was gone, leaving Leonie staring blankly at the empty doorway.

Had he been in town last night? Why hadn't he contacted her? And this appointment with Jack? Was Alex here on business?

Two voices battled in her head—one questioning, the other answering. She'd been out last night. And he usually travelled for business reasons—hadn't he rung her from Boston, from Edinburgh and Paris? So why shouldn't he travel to Rainbow Bay? Why not have an appointment with Jack?

Her heart contracted, but her mind scolded its folly. Dreams were dreams but, if she considered the situation rationally, anything permanent between them was as impossible from her side as it was unlikely from his.

Her body told her that it didn't care about the questions or the answers—reality or dreams. Soft, seductive words had awakened it from a long, celibate sleep and one deep kiss had freed the hormone-fed demons of desire, now cavorting madly through it.

She sighed. It would be simpler if it returned to its normal docility and obedience—like a faithful dog she could trust to 'sit' and 'stay'!

'What can I do for you? Some filing?' Sally slipped into the office. 'You don't want to tire yourself out so much you won't enjoy your holiday.'

Leonie looked blankly at the young office girl.

'Holiday!' Sally repeated helpfully. 'Thing you have when you don't come in to work each day. You're off to the Picnic Races in the morning, aren't you? That should be fun.'

She nodded a vague agreement, wondering how she was ever going to get her mind sufficiently focussed to complete the work she knew must be finished today. With a valiant effort she forced Alex—and the ramifications of his presence in the office—from her mind and concentrated on what had to be done.

'Come back in an hour,' she said. 'I'll have some of this sorted out by then and know what's what.'

Sally retreated, and Leonie attacked the first pile of paper.

She had cleared enough space on her desk to accommodate the cup of coffee Sally brought in for her an hour later.

'Jack wants to see you but I told him to wait until later,' Sally told her as she picked up the filing Leonie had set to one side of the desk.

'Ask him to give me another hour to sort these requisitions into order,' Leonie suggested, although the mention of Jack had brought Alex back to the forefront of her mind and the demons back to life in her body.

Sit! Stay! she told them fiercely.

'Would you mind acting as nurse at the races?' Jack asked as he came briskly into her office exactly one hour later.

Leonie looked up at him, and shook her head.

'Not in the slightest, as long as no one needs nursing when I'm supposed to be presenting ribbons to winners.'

Jack chuckled, but the request was puzzling Leonie.

'We'll have a plane and other medical staff out there, won't we?'

She saw Jack nod, and tried to think who had offered to go to Talgoola Picnic Races this year.

'Nick's going as doctor, with Allysha flying him,' he explained, 'but I like to have a nurse there as well in case the plane has to bring someone back to town. It was to be Susan this year, but with Lachlan still needing care—'

Leonie felt a shiver of fear trickle, like iced water, down her spine. Susan and Eddie Stone, head nurse and chief pilot, were the longest serving staff at Rainbow Bay. Their son, Lachlan, had been injured in a white-water rafting accident and, although he was recovering well, Leonie couldn't help wondering how she would have reacted if it had been her son, Mitchell, who'd lain so still and white in the hospital bed. The accident to one of their RFDS 'family' had made her children doubly precious to her.

'. . .so if you wouldn't mind doubling up a bit. You shouldn't have to do much—it will only be if Nick has to leave. The Army has competent first-aid people who will man the tent while you're at the official functions, and the ambulance from Hopewell will cover the track.'

She forgot her morbid fancies and assured Jack that she would be happy to manage the first aid facility whenever her services were required.

'You should have said no,' Kelly told her, arriving in time to hear her agreeing. 'It'll mean you have less time to spend with that gorgeous man!'

Jack looked bewildered and it was Leonie's turn to chuckle. That puzzled look on Jack's face had become increasingly familiar since Kelly had swept into his life, startling him out of his preoccupation with work.

'You and Alex?' he muttered, one eyebrow rising in disbelief.

Heat folded through Leonie's body and she stumbled into a morass of half-sentences, denying such an assumption.

'Yellow roses!' Kelly said kindly to Jack, winking at Leonie over his shoulder. 'Been bowls of them in her office ever since I arrived at Rainbow Bay! Now, you never send me flowers!'

'Send you flowers? I should beat you every second day—'

'Now that might be fun,' Kelly teased, dodging the hand that reached out to tug at her hair.

Leonie watched them sparring with each other, and envied the love that shone like a nimbus in the air around them.

'There's nothing in it, Kelly,' she said severely, then added, 'Now, get out of here, both of you. It's a wonder any work gets done in this place. . .'

Her voice trailed away as Alex appeared in the doorway behind them.

'We're gone,' Kelly said, seeing him at the same moment and dragging Jack towards the door. 'Enjoy the races, and the rest of your holiday!'

She winked again, and for a moment Leonie wanted to be young and carefree once more—to forget her responsibilities and give herself up to the pleasure she knew she could share with Alex. Not that he'd asked. . .

'I came to ask if you would have dinner with me this evening,' he said, his speech patterns making the request oddly formal.

She looked at his strong, solid figure, imagining the skin and bones and tissues beneath his dark shirt and tailored trousers. The demons, ignoring her commands, danced faster—whirling through her body.

'I'd be delighted,' she said, and smiled at him. Could she pretend to be young and carefree? For one night? For one weekend? For however long he was here?

The demons leapt higher!

'What are you doing for the remainder of the day?' she asked, hoping that she sounded like an efficient business person, not a breathless teenager.

'I have to see the people at the university who conducted the blood tests at Coorawalla. They eliminated many possible sources of the encephalitis. I have a team flying out next week, and I don't want my scientists to be going over the same work.'

Leonie remembered his last visit had coincided with an outbreak of Murray Valley Encephalitis on Coorawalla, one of the island settlements in their RFDS area.

Was Alex's European-based drug company serious about pursuing an inoculation against the virus? Was that reason enough for him to return to the Bay? Common sense told her that it was a more logical reason than a little light seduction!

'Jack was telling me that the university will let my staff use their facilities,' Alex added, and smiled at her. 'I am grateful for the work he has done on my behalf.'

'Not nearly as grateful as we, and all the people in the north, will be if you can locate the carrier of the live virus and develop an inoculation against it.'

They continued to talk about the rare viral encephalitis which had struck the island community. Talking easily—

like old friends—but Leonie felt the unsaid words strung like beads of dew beneath the sentences.

'Going out, Mum? Aren't you leaving for the Picnic Races at dawn tomorrow?'

Mitchell had arrived home as she was giving last-minute instructions to Caroline, and she had to smile at the hint of admonition in his voice.

'Think I need an early night to cope with such stress?' she teased. 'I thought you were the one who finds it hard to get out of bed before midday—not me!'

He responded with a flashing smile, and her heart squeezed with gratitude that these two teenagers she'd reared were becoming her friends. Just when the transition had occurred she wasn't certain, but somewhere along the way, with Mitchell in particular, the mother-child relationship had diminished, to be replaced by a heart-warming—and precious—camaraderie.

It was one of the things she most dreaded losing! One of the things that made her wary of any involvement with Alex. That, and the peace of mind she'd finally managed to salvage from the wreck of her marriage!

'So, where are you going? What lucky charity is getting your support tonight? Or is it more Base business? You let that place run your life, you know.'

Mitchell had taken two strides to the kitchen while she was thinking, and was now engaged in making peanut-butter sandwiches. She knew that food preparation demanded his total concentration so she said, in as casual a voice as she could muster, 'Actually, I'm meeting Alex Solano for dinner.'

'Oh, is he back?' Mitchell asked easily, his attention

focussed on the thickness of the spread. 'Did Carlos come? Will we see them?'

He twisted the bread wrapper into a ball and tossed it across the kitchen divider at Caroline, adding teasingly, 'Will Caro see Carlos?'

Leonie relaxed. Mitchell had read nothing into this 'meeting for dinner'. Was she worrying unnecessarily? Were her fears that he would resent her involvement with a man unfounded? Perhaps she should have talked to them about her feelings for this man, who'd met her so briefly but had then kept in touch. Yet what could she have said? And wouldn't talking about it have diminished her dreams?

'I'll be gone before you're both up in the morning,' she said, concentrating on practical matters. 'Gran will come over before lunch and she'll cook your dinner so I expect you to be here to eat it, Mitchell!'

He looked up from arranging his sandwiches on a plate and gave her a hurt smile.

'Now, you know I'd never miss one of Gran's roast dinners. Off you go and stop fussing. Caro and I will survive the weekend without you. Haven't I been telling you we can manage on our own?'

'With Gran, supplying food and doing your washing,' Leonie reminded him.

'She loves doing it,' Mitchell argued, 'and we love having her here. So why don't you go away somewhere for your holiday—it's not too late to arrange something. Go to one of the islands, or take a cruise. Think of it—lying in the sun, being waited on. It would do you good to live it up a little!'

'I might find myself a man on a tropical island or

a cruise,' she said lightly—testing the waters.

Mitchell's grey eyes, so like her own, darkened, but he obliged with the age-appropriate hoots of laughter.

'Well, I think it would be nice for Mum if she found a man,' Caroline said earnestly.

The laughter stopped and the smiling lips set into a firm line.

'She doesn't need a man!' Mitchell told his sister. 'She's got us, and Gran, and her work! What time has she got for a man?'

'Alex Solano is a man,' Caroline pointed out, for once standing up to the brother she adored.

'Alex Solano is a jet-setting millionaire who probably has ravishingly beautiful and very expensive mistresses stashed in every corner of the world. What would he want with Mum?'

The derisive scorn cut through to her heart.

So much for my son being a friend! Leonie thought, fending off the pain. Then she remembered that friends were people who could speak the truth to you.

She forced a brighter than usual smile on to her lips as she left them. Mitchell's words had given form to her own undefined fears and, although she didn't believe there would be a multitude of women in Alex's life, she was certain that a man as handsome and virile as he would not be likely to practise celibacy.

As she drove into town the tentative delight and anticipation she'd experienced earlier shrivelled inside her.

He was waiting for her in the lobby of the Bay Hotel, and her body ignored the echoes of Mitchell's firm young voice, and warmed at the sight of him.

Striding swiftly towards her, he took hold of her hands

while his gaze travelled slowly from the top of her head to the tip of her toes.

'So beautiful!' he murmured, half smiling and shrugging one shoulder. 'More alluring than I remembered, with your shining silver-blonde hair, your serene, dark-lashed eyes and smooth pale skin.'

She knew she should accept the compliments as nothing more than effusive European courtesy, but the words, the deprecating smile and the impulses from his body all contributed to leave her breathless. She studied him in silence until a slight pressure from his fingers reminded her that they were standing in the middle of a busy lobby and probably attracting attention.

'Come, I've booked a table in the Reef Bistro.'

He steered her towards the lifts which would take them up to the fifteenth floor and the restaurant with spectacular views out over the bay.

Other guests and diners bustled their way into the ornately decorated compartment, and social chatter filled the air. Leonie felt Alex draw her closer against his side to protect her from the crush of bodies, and she was content to stay there, feeling the texture of his body through the layers of their clothes.

'You know I have dreamed of this so many times,' he murmured when they were settled at the table, their meal ordered and wine glasses in hand. 'Sitting here in this perfect place and lifting my glass to toast your soft, seductive eyes—so serious, yet deep with feeling. . .' he paused, raised his glass and sipped deliberately from his drink '. . .and your so, so sensuous lips!'

Again his glass lifted and touched Leonie's in an unspoken salute. It's a game, and he's a master of it, she reminded herself, but she was mesmerised by the movement of his lips as he sipped the wine.

Over the rim of the glass his eyes seduced her, stripping away her defences as her body responded to the silent sexuality of his gaze. Her fingers tightened on the stem of the wine glass until, fearing that the tension would snap it, she set it down carefully on the table.

His hand reached out and covered her fingers, and she felt them tremble beneath that undemanding touch. The demons were unleashed inside her and her body ached for a solace she hadn't known she needed.

'Eat your dinner,' he said a little later, releasing her hand.

She stared blankly at the meal on the table in front of her, unable to remember the waiter bringing it.

Let's forget the meal and go up to your room, she wanted to say, but some minute remnant of sanity prevailed and she bent her head over the meal and pretended to eat.

The silence gnawed its way through her body, straining nerves already taut with unfamiliar emotions. She glanced across the table, but Alex was concentrating on his lobster and not about to start a polite conversation.

'Is Carlos with you?'

She blurted out the question, trying to recapture her usual ease in social situations.

Alex looked up and smiled.

'He's coming later. He'll be joining us at Coorawalla.'

'Us? Your research team? You're staying on with them at Coorawalla?'

The questions seemed to hover between them, then he

nodded briefly while his dark eyes revealed nothing beyond a teasing sensuality.

She should have felt relief that he'd not be in Rainbow Bay for the month he'd mentioned, but her reaction felt more like disappointment.

'Is he well?' she persisted, although she knew from their phone conversations that he was completely recovered from the episode of the bends which had brought the Flying Doctor Service into his life, and Alex into hers.

'He's extremely well, and looking forward to returning to Australia,' Alex assured her, his eyes now twinkling with laughter. 'And Mitchell and Caroline? They are well?'

If you want to play this game I will join you in it, his expression told her.

'Mitchell and Caroline. . .'

She couldn't finish the sentence, but looked across the table at him, her uncertainty so strong she wondered if he could see it.

'They're well. . .'

'But you're worried about them?' he asked, his voice so gentle that she forgot about the mistresses and let her demons loose. 'About their reaction to our relationship?'

She opened her lips to question the word, deciding that it was better to be honest about her misgivings, then heard the gasp of horror that issued from them. Two tables away a waiter had been preparing to flambé crêpes for an elderly couple. Without being consciously aware that she was watching him, Leonie had seen him pour the brandy into the shallow pan and was prepared for the blue flame to flare upward.

The waitress who had arrived to pour coffee for the guests was less prepared. Leonie saw the flames rise, then the pot of coffee jerk from the girl's hand and fall back to the table, splattering the guests and knocking over the pan and the small burner. The waiter leapt backwards, the waitress shrieked and then a sheet of flame followed. Leonie thought of gas, but she was already out of her seat and moving towards the injured guests.

'Everyone keep back. You, waiter, bring more ice.'

She heard Alex's voice behind her as she lifted the bottle of wine from their ice bucket and scooped ice into her napkin. The hot coffee had spilled on the woman's arm. She knew that much, and would start there. She stepped over the litter of food and cooking utensils on the floor and reached the woman's side.

A diner at the table behind the couple had thrown the contents of his ice-bucket over the tablecloth and had put out that fire, but Leonie could smell the escaping gas which could be set alight by a carelessly struck flame.

'Can you see the gas burner?' she heard Alex ask, and was relieved when someone answered. 'Turn it off, but handle it carefully—it will be hot.'

Then he moved across to Leonie's patient, speaking reassuringly to the woman as he felt her carotid pulse and draped his jacket around her shoulders.

He lifted the napkin from her arm and said, 'You will have to have this dressed. The manager is calling an ambulance.'

He knotted his napkin around Leonie's to hold the cool damp cloth in place.

The woman looked up at him, her lips working but no sound coming out. Then there was a soft sighing sound from her male companion, and he slumped forward across the table.

Bad heart! That's what the woman had been saying, Leonie realised as Alex felt for a pulse then eased the man from the chair and stretched him on the floor, beginning CPR with such efficiency that she felt no apprehension that he wouldn't succeed.

The onlookers faded away and diners must have been moved because their section of the restaurant was empty by the time the ambulance men appeared.

'No one mentioned heart attack,' one said brusquely. 'I'll go down and get the defibrillator.'

'No!'

Alex's voice stopped him as he turned towards the entrance.

'There's a pulse, and he's breathing. Get him on the stretcher and down to the vehicle. You can connect him to oxygen—that will help.'

Leonie wasn't surprised to see the men obey Alex's commands. Both his voice and bearing radiated authority.

'He'll be OK,' she murmured to the woman, who was shaking with pain and tension in spite of Alex's warm jacket. 'Are you able to walk, or will we wait for them to carry you down?'

'I'd rather walk,' the woman said. 'I want to stay with him.'

Leonie helped her to her feet and supported her as they followed the stretcher. Alex was walking beside his patient, one finger on his neck as he checked that the man's heart was still beating. Once clear of the confined space in the restaurant, the bearers dropped the stretcher's supports so that they could wheel it instead of carrying it. They eased it into the lift and the woman hurried away from Leonie, reaching out to take the man's hand.

'We were celebrating our fifty-fifth wedding anniversary,' she said softly.

Leonie felt tears prickle behind her eyelids, but she smiled a little when Alex reached a comforting arm around the woman's frail shoulders and said, 'He will be all right. Next year you can celebrate fifty-six, but not with crêpes Suzette, I think?'

The ambulance was parked in the basement, and the patient was wheeled straight on board. One of the ambulance men climbed in and attached monitor leads to the elderly man's chest.

Alex nodded his approval, then leant into the vehicle to murmur something to the man.

The second stretcher was tilted upward so that the woman could sit beside her husband.

'Is there someone I can phone for you?' Leonie asked, not wanting to abandon the couple to the mercy of the accident and emergency department.

'My granddaughter is on duty at the hospital tonight,' the woman replied. Momentarily forgetting her husband, she smiled with pride. 'She's a doctor there!'

The driver shut the door, and the ambulance moved swiftly and almost silently away.

'She's still wearing your jacket,' Leonie said.

Alex drew her close, and raised one hand to tilt her head up so that he could look into her eyes

'I have another one,' he told her, a funny little smile playing around his lips.

She smiled back, knowing exactly what he was thinking. The sexual tension that had stretched between them so strongly that Leonie had found it impossible to eat had been dampened by the drama, as effectively subdued as the fire had been by the bucket of ice and water.

'Would you like to come up to my room? I could order a sandwich and coffee from room service.'

She looked at him and shook her head. She wasn't superstitious, but she had a sense of having been saved from something and didn't want to tempt fate a second time tonight.

'The plane's leaving at six-thirty,' she reminded him. 'Jack said you were definitely coming. Are you flying out with us?'

He shook his head.

'I flew from Switzerland in the company jet, and my pilot assures me he can find Talgoola so I'll let him have his fun!'

He leant forward and kissed her on the lips.

She stood very still, aware that the tension between them was only dampened—not completely dead.

'You're tired,' he murmured, running his hand through her hair then tracing his fingers down the side of her face. 'There's time ahead for both of us,' he promised, kissing her lightly again.

She felt her body responding and leant into him, but he put his hands on her shoulders and held her upright.

'Where did you park your car? I'll walk you to it,' he said, and his voice sounded husky, as if the words had cost him a great effort.

She started the car, a rueful smile plucking at her lips as she realised that the evening had transpired more or less as Mitchell had imagined it! But as she drove away she glimpsed Alex, waiting on the kerb until she turned the corner, and she fought her own contrary disappointment.

CHAPTER TWO

LIGHTS blazed at the Stones' house, and Leonie slowed the car and then pulled up outside, Alex and the strange evening forgotten as she prayed that Lachlan was all right. Susan answered her quiet knock.

'No, we've been celebrating,' she explained. 'That's why we're up so late. Lachlan went back to school today—only for half a day, but it's a beginning. And what are you doing, roaming the streets at eleven o'clock at night?'

One mention of Alex was enough for Susan. She drew Leonie inside and insisted that she stay for coffee.

'I want to know all!' she warned, and Leonie had to laugh. Susan always wanted to 'know all', but she was a good friend and probably the only person she could talk to about her dilemma.

'So, what do I do?' she asked, when she had explained about Alex's return to the Bay, Mitchell's derision and her own uncertainty about the situation.

'Physically, do you want him?' Susan asked in her blunt nurse's voice.

Leonie felt her cheeks grow warm, but she forced herself to reply with equal candour.

'Desperately, I think!' She nearly choked on the words but had to continue. 'I didn't think I'd ever feel this way! I know it's only sexual—but it aches in me, Susan, and destroys my peace of mind, my resolution! He only has to look at me and I melt! It's ridiculous! Even with Craig

I never felt like this, and I loved him so much.'

Her voice caught on the words, and Susan reached out and patted her on the arm.

'I think you're in need of a bit of good, old-fashioned loving!'

'But if it's only physical it isn't love—it's lust!' Leonie pointed out, and Susan smiled.

'At this stage, seeing how strung up you are, I don't think I'd worry about semantics. You say you can't imagine it leading to anything permanent so why not take what he offers? Have an affair with him—kick up your heels—enjoy yourself!'

'But the kids? What would they think?'

Susan looked pityingly at her.

'They need never know,' she said firmly. 'Do you think Eddie and I put out an announcement to the family every time we make love? All kids assume that their parents are too old for sex. Most of them work out how many children were conceived in the marriage, and take that as the number of times their parents copulated. They don't want to know any more, Leonie!'

She nodded, aware of the truth in Susan's words.

'But there's something uncomfortable about a "secret" affair,' she said. 'It feels sneaky somehow!'

Susan slammed her mug down on the table with unnecessary force.

'For heaven's sake, Leonie! You're not cheating on a husband or a boyfriend—and it won't be any secret to the staff because we've all seen you go gooey every time the roses arrived!'

'I do not go gooey!' Leonie argued, horrified by her own transparency. 'And if the Base knows then the world knows,' she added gloomily. 'So it's impossible. I should go back to the hotel and tell him I'm not interested.'

'If you went back to that hotel you'd end up in bed with him tonight!' Susan warned with uncanny percipience. 'And you're not hiding something from the staff, who will all delight in the fact that you're finally doing something for yourself—instead of concentrating so single-mindedly on your children! Take the chance, Leonie,' she urged. 'Seize it with both hands, and enjoy every wonderful moment of it!'

She paused to sip her coffee, then continued, 'And I will promise you no one outside the staff will ever know. I'll talk to them myself—they'll understand you don't want the kids upset.'

Relief and longing and a strange excitement battled for possession of her mind.

'It's irresponsible though, isn't it?' she said, knowing that it was but wanting to hear Susan deny it.

'It's a chance to snatch a little interlude of pleasure, that's what it is,' Susan told her. 'Irresponsible is getting pregnant. I don't suppose you've thought of that!'

Leonie gasped with shock. In all the rush of hormonal excitement pregnancy had been her last consideration. Now that *was* irresponsible!

'I'll have to go on the Pill,' she muttered. 'I know nothing about the new ones! I found some information when I was talking to Mitchell and Caroline about precautions, but I didn't take much notice of it. How long do they take to work? What will I take? Oh, Susan, I can't go up the road to our family doctor and ask for a prescription!'

Her voice had risen to a wail, and she felt more like fourteen than close to forty!

'The Pill is risky,' Susan told her. 'You should have been on it a month ago. Anyway, he should be the one taking precautions. Don't you preach safe sex to your kids? He's a stranger, after all. Who knows where he's been?'

'Stashed mistresses!' Leonie murmured, calming down in the face of Susan's prosaic statements.

'Stashed what?'

She smiled and said, 'Mitchell says a man as wealthy and good-looking as Alex would have mistresses stashed all over the place.'

Susan cocked her head.

'Does that worry you?'

Leonie thought for a moment, then shrugged.

'The whole thing is so unreal, Susan, that I don't think it does. I mean, I know nothing can ever come of it. As you say, it will be an interlude, that's all.'

She looked at Susan who was studying her intently.

'I can handle that side of it,' she promised her friend. As long as I don't do anything stupid like fall in love with the man! she reminded herself. Then she grinned, and admitted, 'I can handle that much more easily than I can suggest to a man that he must wear a condom! So much for being grown up and confident and self-assured!'

She saw Susan's frown and hurried to assure her.

'I know, I know! Safe sex! I *will* remember!'

She left the Stones' more confused than ever, only certain that the easiest course would be to avoid Alex as much as possible or hope that some beautiful young creature—mistress material—might take his fancy at Talgoola!

Nick was loading supplies and equipment into the plane when Leonie arrived at the airport next morning.

'Allysha's doing her final checks, with a handsome Italian pilot watching every move,' he said tartly.

'Where did the pilot—?'

Nick interrupted with a nod towards the hangar door, and hurried on towards the plane. Leonie smiled as she watched him. He couldn't be jealous when Allysha so obviously adored him.

Then she added the pilot to Nick's gesture and forgot other people's relationships, moving swiftly into the gloomy interior of the huge hangar.

Alex was over by their big emergency plane, inspecting it with professional competence. As she walked towards him he turned, arms opening, so that they met beneath the plane's wing in a tense embrace. She forgot about avoiding him, and prayed that no youthful beauty would swim into his ken at Talgoola!

'I should never have let you go last night,' he murmured in her ear when the initial tremors of excitement had died down.

'It could be like that all weekend,' she reminded him. 'I'm going out there to work, remember.'

He eased her a little way from his body and looked down into her face.

'Then I will have to work with you,' he promised. 'I have waited too long to have you snatched away from my side by the fickleness of fate—or by careless revellers with their cuts and bruises.'

He bent his head and kissed her, emphasising his words with the searing mastery of his lips.

Leonie pulled away, her knees weak with unfulfilled desire.

'I've a plane to catch,' she said, the words coming out

as a breathless whisper because her lungs were behaving badly once again.

He smiled and gave the little shrug she was beginning to recognise.

'And I forget why I'm here!' He took her hand. 'Fly to Talgoola with me? I have spoken to Nick, and he says that's OK.'

He looked down into her face, his brown eyes alight with pleasure. 'Say you will come? Say you will fly with me into your "outback". I have lived a short time in Perth and seen the coastal part of Queensland, but this is my first visit to your inland.'

As he paused she realised how much his enthusiasm, his delight in new experiences, excited her. Somewhere along the path her life had taken she'd lost that enthusiasm and delight—the two things which could make the most ordinary of days special.

'Say you will share the experience with me?'

Beneath the smooth sophisticate in his designer jeans and knitted silk shirt she sensed a boy who craved adventure. It's an interlude, she reminded herself, then she smiled and put her hand in his.

'I'd be delighted,' she told him, and the demons danced again.

The jet was luxurious, compared to the practical and spartan interiors of the RFDS planes, but its opulence was lost on her as she relaxed and enjoyed the pleasure of being with Alex. They sat, hand in hand like children, and peered through the windows.

Seeing her country through Alex's eyes, Leonie thrilled to the green fields of waving cane, then the lush mantle of darker green rainforest that hid the seaward slopes of the ranges.

Farms dotted the plateau, patchwork patterns of green or richest red-brown with golden fields of sunflowers lifting their faces to the sun.

'So much land, so much space,' Alex murmured as the farms gave way to grazing properties.

They were over eucalypt scrub country where cattle grazed at will between the yearly musters. Then the trees grew smaller, became stunted bushes and the round grey blobs of salt-bush. This was sheep country, rich with grass after rain, but today so bare and brown that it was hard to believe any animal could exist there.

'There are huge letters and numbers painted on the roof of that house,' he pointed out.

'It's their radio call sign,' Leonie replied, explaining about the pedal radios, the only form of communication in the bush fifty years ago. 'It's only recently that outback areas have come under a satellite phone link. In fact, a few of our people still rely on radio for contact.'

They were deep in a discussion of the ramifications of providing a medical service over such a vast area when Alex pointed ahead.

'Look, look!' he said, slipping his arm around her shoulders and drawing her closer to the window. 'There—in the middle of nowhere—hundreds of planes.'

'That's Talgoola,' Leonie told him, smiling at his excitement.

'But where's the town?'

They were circling now and he peered downward, searching for something he couldn't see.

'There is no town,' she explained, 'apart from the hotel and a couple of ruined cottages.'

'No town? But this is a big race meeting! Why have it in a place where there are no people?'

She chuckled.

'You've seen the planes. If you look out the other side you'll see the cars, trucks and buses. There are plenty of people.'

'And they all come to this place to see a horse race?'

'It's become a tourist attraction,' she explained. 'A bit like the running of the bulls at Pamploma—only in the middle of nowhere. Some people might be travelling around the country, and try to be at Talgoola for the races. Others make the trip especially because they want to experience the atmosphere.'

'The atmosphere?' Alex cast a dubious glance out of the window at the flat, barren plains beneath them. 'At least Pamploma has a town.'

'And, for four days every year, Talgoola has a town,' she pointed out. 'A tent town!'

They swooped lower over the bright butterfly colours of the camping area, the neat lines of caravans and the trucks loaded with food and drink for the revellers.

The wheels touched the ground, and the jet flew past what looked like a battalion of parked planes.

'I have no tent. I thought. . .'

'Didn't Jack explain? We have beds in the first-aid tent—you can sleep in there with me,' Leonie offered, chuckling quietly at the thought of Alex on one of the narrow stretchers they kept to use at Picnic Races, 'and your pilot, and whatever patients we happen to be keeping in overnight!'

He turned towards her, his dark eyes glowing.

'I can wait a little longer,' he promised, in a voice that almost denied the words, 'as long as we are together, learning things about each other.' He slid his fingers along her arm. 'Touching—like this!' He leant towards her. 'Kissing—like this!'

He's a practised seducer, she reminded herself, but then his lips closed on hers and she felt the burning flame of his desire—banked fires, building in heat and intensity as they waited to be released.

The Plane's speed dropped and they taxied across rougher, more uneven ground. She pulled away from him. She would give in to this madness he conjured to life within her—she knew that as well as she knew that the sun would set. But she was no longer a silly teenager lost in dreams of love—she was a mature woman with a stable and secure life.

She knew she had to stand up to his mastery, to make her own terms in this relationship, so that she could survive the experience unscathed—so she could protect her peace of mind and her relationship with her children. But how?

'So?' he asked, and she pretended to misunderstand, hiding her emotional indecision behind her calm, competent Base Manager manner.

'Someone is showing the pilot where he can park,' she explained. 'It has to be highly organised or the situation could descend into chaos.'

Through the window she saw the RFDS plane. She pointed to it, explaining to Alex that it was the only plane permitted to remain on the runway—ready for a quick take-off, should an emergency occur.

A garishly painted, open-topped Jeep was pulled up

nearby, and she could see Nick and Allysha unloading equipment into the vehicle.

'That's our ambulance,' she explained to Alex. 'The publican owns it and he repaints it every year especially for us.'

'It will stand out,' Alex agreed, and Leonie sensed that his desire had been diverted into excitement for this new experience. It was his way, she realised, to be totally involved in whatever he was doing—whether making love or learning the ways of a foreign country! Slowly the 'businessman' image was being stripped away, leaving a 'man of action' in its place!

'Want a lift?'

The 'ambulance' pulled up as they descended from the plane. Nick was driving and he waved his hand towards the mounds of equipment behind him.

'You can sit on top of that lot or wait until I come back for Allysha. I'll get your pilot at the same time. Seems they have to tie things down and cover the air holes—technical stuff like that!'

Alex was smiling as he turned to Leonie and lifted her into the air. She was conscious of his hands against her waist, then of being swung, with little ceremony, onto the top of the baggage.

'I will tell my pilot and come with you,' he said to Nick, and darted back up the steps.

'You'd think a guy like him would be horrified to find himself at this kind of show, but he's as excited as a kid let out of school,' Nick remarked, his fingers tapping out a little tune on the steering-wheel.

'And you're not?' Leonie asked.

He turned and grinned at her.

'I am!' he admitted. 'I've visited Talgoola before but this is the first time I've come to the races. I've been to smaller Picnic Races in New South Wales, but this and Birdsville are the most well known.'

Alex returned and they set off for the 'town', Leonie pointing out the features to the two 'newcomers'.

'We have the favoured spot right behind the hotel, and can use their bathroom and toilet facilities. When you see the water tankers with bush showers rigged up, and chemical toilets dotted through the camping area, you'll understand how privileged we are.'

'And is our tent here in the baggage? Do we erect it ourselves?'

Leonie smiled to herself. How quickly he had become one of 'us'! And how seductive the change in him was! Did he know that? Do it deliberately?

'The tent, like the ambulance, belongs to the publican and fortunately we don't have to erect it ourselves.'

'The race meeting has become so well known that the Army uses it as an exercise, and their hefty lads do a lot of the heavy work.' Nick took up the explanation. 'They also manage the parking of land vehicles and planes, and take care of hygiene in the camping area.'

He slowed down as they approached the low-set building that was Talgoola's hotel and village centre and then, with Leonie directing him, turned onto a rough track and stopped beside a large tent, brightened by spray-painted graffiti.

'One first-aid tent!' Leonie announced.

Alex slid from his perch on top of the equipment and reached up to lift Leonie down. Her feet found the ground, but he held her for a moment longer. Again the feeling of being thrust back to adolescence rushed through her and she glanced towards Nick, wondering whether he had noticed. But did it matter if he did?

Alex's fingers brushed across her forehead, as if to smooth away her concern, then he linked his fingers through hers and turned to Nick.

'I am trying to persuade this woman to fall—just a little—in love with me,' he announced, startling Nick so much that he dropped the sleeping bag he had hauled from the pile.

'Ah!' Nick shifted from one foot to the other with all the embarrassment of an Australian male confronted with outspoken statements of affection.

Then he smiled and said, 'Well, good luck to you. They don't come any better than Leonie!'

She felt the heat creeping up her neck, and busied herself with the baggage.

'But if you do the wrong thing by her,' Nick continued in conversational tones, 'you'll have any number of furious RFDS staff members out for your blood.'

'Hey, I'm standing here while you two are discussing my personal business!' she pointed out, lifting her flaming face to glare at Nick. 'And I'm thirty-eight years old and should be able to look after myself—if I wanted to fall in love with anyone, that is! Which I don't, of course. . .' The confused flow of words faltered to a halt before she gathered her wits, and Nick looked thoroughly confused as he hurried away.

'Not want to fall in love?' Alex asked, taking the bags she'd liberated from the pile and leaning forward to kiss her on the nose. 'Will you also deny the attraction between us?' he added, following her into the tent.

She put down the cases she had carried and turned towards him. The man of adventure was infinitely more approachable than the sophisticate, but she didn't trust this sudden change in mood and tactics.

'I couldn't deny that,' she said soberly, looking into the face that seemed to smile especially for her. 'But it's nothing to do with love, Alex!'

His eyes darkened but she was too busy searching for the words she needed to wonder why. 'And I'm not used to—'

'You don't like me taking your hand, holding your arm—standing close so we are touching each other?'

The desire-deepened words made her feel weak and trembly and she knew she couldn't lie.

'I do like it,' she muttered, her eyes pleading for him to understand. 'But it's new to me—different! Hard to handle all at once! It's me I'm uncomfortable with, Alex, not you. It's my own reactions I'm having difficulty... controlling or assimilating... I don't know!'

'I'll go along with this courtship stuff as long as no one shirks their duty,' Nick told them, striding into the tent and dropping an armload of gear on the ground. 'I know you're on holidays, Leonie, and Alex is our guest but there's work to be done. The sooner everything's set up the sooner we can go and join the festivities. Besides, I want that Jeep unloaded so I can get back to the airfield before Alex's pilot starts flirting with my wife.'

They hurried out to collect the remainder of the equipment, then watched as Nick roared off towards the airfield.

'First patient!' a voice called, and Leonie looked up to see a soldier supporting a young man who was limping towards them.

She grabbed a chair from a pile stacked on the hotel

verandah and set it in the shade outside the tent.

'Sit for a minute while we unpack what we'll need,' she told him, but Alex was already kneeling on the ground and unwrapping the bloody rag that was wrapped around the young man's foot.

'What happened?' she heard him ask as she scrabbled through their gear for a bowl and antiseptic solution.

'I was hitting a tent peg into the ground with an axe and the—' Leonie shuddered at the expletive '—thing flew off the handle and landed on my foot.'

She crossed to the water tank set up outside the tent and ran water into the basin, then added antiseptic that would sterilise both the water and the wound.

'It needs stitches and your foot should be X-rayed for broken bones,' Alex was saying as she squatted beside him and slid the bowl of water across so that she could clean the dusty, blood-caked foot.

'I'm not leaving this place till after the races,' the man informed him. 'Just wrap it up so the dirt won't get in it and I'll worry about X-rays when I get home.'

Alex looked shocked so Leonie took over.

'I'll clean it up, and Nick will be back shortly,' she said to Alex, not wanting to embroil him in RFDS work before he'd had time to settle in.

'I will clean it up and stitch it,' he insisted, his eyes slanting a smiling look into hers. 'Didn't Nick tell us there was work to be done?'

He was splashing water over the man's foot as he spoke, holding the edges of the gaping wound with one hand.

'You get sutures, internal and external, please—also antibiotic powder, painkiller and, I think, some broad-spectrum antibiotics. Who knows what infections might be in there?'

His crisp commands took Leonie back to her hospital days, and she obeyed automatically, searching through the pile of equipment until she located what he would need.

She placed them on a tray, then realised that he was handling his patient without gloves and searched again until she located a large pair. Dressing packs were in the same case so she pulled out one of those and some waterproof tape. If they could ensure the wound stayed dry there would be less chance of infection.

Returning to his side, she saw his quick, all-encompassing glance, and caught the smile he directed towards her when he saw the gloves.

She pulled on the pair she'd found for herself and said, 'I'll hold the wound while you wash your hands and put on your gloves. You don't want to be infecting this young man with any more germs.'

'Particularly not foreign ones,' Alex agreed seriously, although she could see his lips twitching and knew he realised that she was insisting to protect him, as much as the young man, from possible infection.

He scrubbed his hands quickly and efficiently and was back within minutes to inject the local anaesthetic, then stitch up the wound. He sat back to let Leonie apply the dressing, asking his patient about his tetanus shots.

'So, you do not need a booster but you will take antibiotics,' he said, as the man rose gingerly to his feet. Alex turned to Leonie. 'Do we prescribe, or hand out, or what?'

'We hand out, then hold out our own hand for a donation to the Service,' Leonie told him. 'About a third of the money raised here this weekend is donated to the RFDS so we donate our time and provide medical care.'

The young man had dug in his pocket and produced a five-dollar note which he handed to Alex.

'Most of our patients are happy to make an extra donation, which helps cover the costs of drugs and dressings.'

She wrote him a receipt and watched him limp away, then turned to smile at Alex.

'I told you they wouldn't get any work done, Allysha!' Nick's voice echoed through the canvas 'home'. 'They're still standing exactly where I left them, smiling at each other over the pile of gear.'

'I'll have you know I've dealt with your first customer, *and* been paid for it!'

Alex fluttered the note towards Nick, then waved his hand towards the doorway where the bowl and medical waste were further evidence of his industry. Nick conceded his error and led Alex outside to show them the sealed containers they used for waste disposal.

Leonie bent over the equipment, her heart bubbling with happiness. To be doing a job she enjoyed, at a place she loved, with someone special! Sharing these simple pleasures! Surely that was as good as you could get in this life.

Not quite as good, her body reminded her as the musical sound of Alex's deep laugh fuelled the fires within her. She thrust away a fleeting image of Mitchell's disapproving face. It was one weekend—two days and two nights—surely she was entitled to that!

Within an hour the folding camp stretchers had been made up in the rear section of the tent, and a smaller tent for Nick and Allysha had been erected outside. One of the stretchers from the plane was set up on its supporting legs to act as an examination table, while the other was lashed firmly in the back of the Jeep and covered with a tarpaulin.

Drugs and equipment had been sorted and stacked in neat array along a trestle table to one side of the entrance, and chairs were in position both outside and inside the shelter. Their Army helper had strung insulated electricity cables from the hotel to the tent to provide power for lights, their small freezer and an electric kettle.

'We eat at the hotel,' Allysha explained to Nick and Alex, 'or, if you're over at the racetrack, you can buy yourself a snack. There's tea and coffee here, cold drinks in the cool box.'

'So, now we can go exploring?'

CHAPTER THREE

NICK was as excited as Alex, Leonie realised, but as the others piled into the vehicle she crossed to 'their' soldier and told him where they were going and when they expected to return. She also gave him a card with the phone number of her mobile printed on it.

'He will guard the tent?' Alex asked as she clambered into the back and sat beside him on the hard metal bench. He sounded amused.

'He'll keep an eye on things for us,' she replied. 'We can't leave the tent unoccupied because of the drugs.'

They were driving through the camping area now, and Alex's attention was diverted by the number of people strolling around, chatting to each other or beginning their 'party', cans of beer in their hands. Beyond the tents were the caravans, a different generation of revellers but seemingly as excited as the younger tourists.

'The racetrack's over there to our right,' Allysha, who was driving, pointed out. 'We'll go this way, and see where the horses are kept.'

'It's like another township,' Alex said in awe as they drove through neat rows of horse boxes. The animals were tethered outside their boxes, most of them contentedly munching on the wisps of lucerne stuffed into the feed bags that hung above their heads.

'That's a pacifier, rather than a feed for them,' Allysha explained. 'If there'd been rain they would have been hobbled and turned out to graze, but with no grass they'd get bored.'

'They are strong, solid-looking animals,' Alex remarked.

Leonie explained.

'Traditionally, the horses raced at Picnic Races were the best work horses on a property. The tradition began exactly as the name suggests—a group of local people getting together to have a picnic. Each stockman or property owner would bring along his best horse, and the races between them would provide the day's entertainment.'

'So they are not racehorses?'

'They shouldn't be,' Allysha told him, 'although these days, with horses being used less for everyday work on farms and properties, many people are breeding the faster horses.'

'And there's a minimum, not maximum, weight limit,' Leonie added, 'because many of the riders are amateurs.'

They were approaching the racetrack itself now, and Nick pointed out the scaffolding being erected to make extra viewing stands.

'Will they be finished in time for the first race?' Alex glanced at his watch. 'It's ten o'clock now!'

'They'll be finished,' Leonie assured him, while Allysha wove the 'ambulance' along a narrow passage between the mobile food stalls and over towards where sideshow rides gave the outer area a carnival appearance.

'Can we get out and walk about, or should we return to the tent?' Alex asked.

'You are a guest and Leonie is only on standby duty,' Nick told him as Allysha stopped the car. 'I'll go back to the tent, and all three of you can have a wander around.'

'Me wander around?' Allysha exclaimed. 'You know me better than that, Nick Grant! I fly or I drive.'

'She probably wants first shower,' Nick added, but Leonie wondered if they were being tactful.

Not that it mattered, she decided a little later as she walked arm in arm with Alex through the fairgrounds. The sun was warm on her bare arms and legs, and she could feel anticipation buzzing like an insect in the air around them.

'It is most amazing that so many people come so far,' Alex said. He paused and drew her out of the way of a motor-scooter, threading its way through the stalls.

'You have probably come further than most,' she reminded him, relishing the heat of their closeness.

He touched her hair, then his fingers lingered on her skin and the soft pad of his thumb brushed against her mouth. Her lips opened, a silent gasp, and she felt desire burn deep in her stomach.

'I had another reason,' he whispered, then the noise and bustle of their surroundings broke over them like a wave and they moved on through the thickening crowds, making their way back to the tent.

Leonie scolded herself, dismayed at how easily he could arouse her. Lack of privacy and uncomfortable stretchers might keep them apart over this weekend, but she didn't know if she was glad or sorry.

Have an affair with the man, and enjoy it, her physical self urged. Forget the past, forget the kids—steal whatever time the two of you might have together from your other life and live it purely for the pleasure it can bring. She repeated the words both she and Susan had said before, but they were so foreign to her nature that she found them unconvincing.

'Changing of the guard,' Alex joked, and she came out of her reverie to see two soldiers outside the big tent.

'First-aid officers,' she explained. 'They will stay here while we're at the races.'

'Do they mind missing all the fun?'

She smiled at the concern in his voice. She loved the way he became instantly involved in what was happening around him, even to the point of caring how others might feel.

'There are more races tomorrow. They will be replaced by two other qualified men and enjoy the second day's fun.'

Allysha appeared from the direction of the hotel, faultlessly attired in a cream linen suit with a bright, autumn-toned silk blouse beneath it. A cream felt broad-brimmed cowboy-style hat completed her ensemble, and Alex whistled softly as she stepped carefully across the dusty ground towards the tent.

'So, it is that kind of party?' he murmured, turning towards Leonie with his eyes glowing.

'Don't people get dressed up to go to the races in Italy and Switzerland?' she retorted. 'I'm heading for the shower now Allysha's finished. Nick will point you in the right direction for the men's.'

She hurried into the tent and picked up the plastic suit-bag that held her two good outfits. With the clothes, a towel, and her toiletry bag she headed back towards the hotel.

'Nick and I will leave shortly,' Allysha told her. 'I want to go over to the Army's radio base for a weather report. We'll take Alex's pilot with us—he's dressed and raring to go! Do you want us to come back for you and Alex or will you walk?'

'A weather report?' Leonie looked up into the cloudless blue sky. A desultory wind was flapping the bunting stretched across the ridge of the hotel roof, but the weather was as close to perfect as she could imagine.

'There are winds getting up in the west,' Allysha explained. 'The rumour is that they could strengthen and bring dust.'

Dust was normal at these big events when years of drought had left the country denuded of all covering, but wind and dust was a different matter. A dust storm could sweep across the empty plains, blotting out the sun and pouring its particles into every minute corner of whatever stood in its way.

'We'll walk over,' Leonie assured her. 'And keep our fingers crossed that the dust is an unfounded rumour!'

She showered quickly and dressed, pleased with the smart black and white suit she'd bought especially for today's races. She adjusted the scrap of black lace that showed above the buttons of the jacket and smoothed moisturiser and a light brush of powder over her face. Although officially spring the days were hot, and too much make-up would look heavy and unnatural.

Searching through her toiletry bag, she found the new scarlet lipstick and brushed its colour onto her normally pale lips. It exactly matched the red feather on her snug-fitting black hat. She stood back and surveyed at herself in the bathroom's ancient mirror.

Not bad at all!

'You look charming!' Alex exclaimed when she

returned to the tent and found him chatting to the two soldiers. She fought the blush!

'I've an important role to play this afternoon,' she informed him, taking his arm for support as her high heels picked their way over the rough ground. 'I'm the official face of the RFDS and have to present the prizes for the main race.'

'So, this elegance is for business reasons, not for me?' he murmured, as they joined the throng moving towards the track. 'Even this cheeky snippet of lace?'

His fingers touched the skin between her breasts and she shivered in the hot sunshine, wanting him so desperately that she was shaken by the need.

Turning towards him, she looked into his face and read an answering hunger in his eyes.

'This is mad,' she muttered. 'I should have stopped it ages ago—should have told you not to phone, not to send the flowers, not to come!'

'But why is it madness, Leonie?' he asked, his dark brows drawn together in perplexity. 'We are a man and a woman, both unattached, and strongly attracted to each other. We are mature adults, granted a glimpse—a taste—of something special. It is our right to explore it to see where it might lead.'

She shifted uneasily, a small smile tugging at her lips although part of her felt like crying.

'You make it sound almost like a duty!' she teased, but won no answering smile from his lips or from the dark eyes that looked so steadily into hers.

'It could be that,' he said soberly. 'Is it not our duty to make the most of the life we have been given—to use it well, not squander its opportunities?'

The noise of the loudspeaker, announcing the field for the first race, intruded into their conversation before she could explain her fears, and they walked on to find their places among the officials in the main stand.

The crowd grew thicker, a mass of people dressed in everything from bikinis to top hats and tails. Leonie watched Alex as he absorbed the strange spectacle, intent on the behaviour of such a diverse group all gathered in this barren landscape to watch not very good horses race each other.

'It's the meeting with other people—the party atmosphere, not the races—that draws them here,' he said a little later.

'Not all of them,' she argued, waving towards the bookmakers' stands where the gambling fever held sway.

People pressed around them, edging their bodies closer—intensifying an inner excitement that was echoed in the bugle call announcing the first race.

'If you don't want to have a bet let's get up into the stand. It might be slightly less crowded,' Leonie shouted above the din.

'Not enjoying this?' His eyes teased her senses, challenging her to deny her responsiveness. She felt the tell-tale heat in her cheeks, but found the determination to seize his hand and drag him towards the relative decorum of the stands.

The first race was under way, with a real ambulance following the horses on an inner track.

'So, your brightly painted machine is a joke?' Alex asked.

'It's more a back-up,' Leonie explained. 'This one comes from Hopewell, the nearest town. It's three hours by road, and has a hospital which can handle fractures and the minor injuries. We fly out more serious injuries, or medical emergencies, and provide back-up if the ambulance isn't here.'

He frowned and looked around at the cheering crowds, the thundering horses.

'So, do you expect a great deal of trouble that you have such extensive medical cover?'

She laughed and shook her head.

'Look at it, Alex! Feel it! See out there, beyond the planes, there's nothing. Thousands of kilometres of nothing, yet the spirit of these people and their forefathers conquered that emptiness. The races are a celebration of that spirit, and a reminder for city folk of what the bush is like. People love coming—even doctors, nurses, base managers and ambulance drivers! The moment this ambulance radios that it's heading back to town with passengers another one leaves town to take its place.'

He looked around and she could almost feel his awareness growing as he considered the special wonder of the gathering, seeing it as the salute it was to the people who endured such isolation and loneliness to make a living in this harsh country.

'We've room over here for you two.' Nick attracted their attention and led them towards the centre of the stand where Allysha was guarding three seats. 'I'm going down to have a bet. Want me to put money on something for you?'

He turned to Leonie, who glanced down to where the winners of the first race were parading.

'I'll have a dollar on number four,' she told Nick, finding a coin in her handbag and passing it to him.

'I'll come with you,' Alex told him, then turned to Leonie. 'What do you know about number four?' he asked suspiciously.

She smiled sweetly at him.

'It comes after number three,' she said, and waved him away.

He frowned at her but finally turned to hurry after Nick.

'Men take this betting business far too seriously,' Allysha remarked as Leonie settled herself in one of the reserved seats. 'Nick frowned exactly like that when I asked him to put my dollar on Red Robin.'

'For the colour?' Leonie asked.

'No, I had a dog called Robin once. It was a red kelpie.'

They watched the horses parade, laughing when they realised that Red Robin was carrying the number four. The trumpet sounded and the horses left the parade area in front of the stand, cantering towards the starting position on the other side of the track.

Nick and Alex returned, both looking pleased with themselves after getting a good price on the favourite—a showy black gelding called Lightning. The race began and the crowd rose to their feet, voices crying out to horses who couldn't hear.

The glossy coat of the favourite showed him to be in the lead at the turn, but a wall of horses closed on him and a big, shaggy chestnut surged to the front and then drew away from them. The crowd noise lessened as anxious eyes sought Lightning, but Leonie and Allysha cheered themselves hoarse as Red Robin dashed past the winning post.

'It was a hundred to one!' Nick complained.

'It should not have had any chance,' Alex added, but

he turned to Leonie and handed her the race-book. 'So,' he said, 'you will pick the next one for me!'

She laughed and shook her head.

'I've had my bet for the day,' she told him. 'One hundred lovely dollars. I might even pay for the tickets for tonight's dinner.'

'If it's still on,' Allysha told her, as their excitement simmered down. 'The weather bureau puts us on track for a dust storm. I'm checking in again at four, and if it's still heading this way I won't risk the plane. Although we use covers on the air intakes, you can't keep storm dust out of the engines. I'd fly back to Base or across to Mt Isa, and wait there for an emergency call.'

'I didn't realise it might be that serious,' Leonie told her. 'Would Nick stay?'

Allysha grinned.

'Could you see him leaving?' she asked. 'Some people might see this as a great big party, but he sees it as one huge potential disaster. I should have realised he'd react this way before I persuaded Jack to let us come this year. He actually checked the scaffolding under this stand before he let me sit up here.'

Leonie chuckled. Nick was a dedicated, committed doctor, but he was also a worrier.

The next race began before the two men returned, and Leonie was looking for Alex's figure in the crowd when a horse crashed through the inner barrier. Allysha's shocked cry and pointing finger made her look towards the racetrack in time to see the rider being flung in an arc through the air.

The ambulance drew up beside the ominously still body, and the noise of the crowd cheering the favourite as he took the honours told Leonie that few people had seen the accident. Two men raced across the track—Nick and Alex.

'Should we make our way down?' Leonie asked, but Allysha shook her head.

'The ambulance man knows to signal in this direction if he needs a doctor or a plane. If I go down lower I might miss that.'

They watched, their hearts thumping, not knowing if a signal would be good news or bad. The attendant slid a stretcher from the ambulance, and Alex helped him carry it towards the fallen rider. Minutes later the ambulance man stood up and waved a red card towards the stands.

'They want to fly him out,' Allysha said, and began moving down the steps.

'Are you going over there? Will you go to the airfield with the ambulance?' Leonie asked.

'No! I'll take our "ambulance" and go straight to the airfield. That way, I'll have the plane ready for take-off by the time they arrive. Will you let Nick know I'm on my way? If he's going to travel with the patient ask Alex to come out to the airport and drive our vehicle back.'

'I'll come with you and drive it back,' Leonie suggested.

'And who'll present the prizes for the Flying Doctor Handicap?' Allysha asked as they reached the ground and hurried towards the car park. 'Besides, you'll be busy enough tomorrow if we can't get back because of the dust.'

She waved goodbye and Leonie headed towards the track, explaining who she was to an official before she slipped beneath the rail and ploughed her way through the soft sand towards the little group beside the ambulance.

Alex was kneeling by the injured rider, stacking padded dressings on his stomach.

'Nick's going to take the man back to Rainbow Bay,' he said softly. 'We suspect some spinal damage, and a piece of the railing has penetrated his abdomen.'

Nausea tightened her stomach as she realised what Alex was doing. He was packing dressings around the piece of timber, securing it so that it couldn't move when the man was shifted. Leonie watched him tape the dressings firmly into place. She knew this was the correct procedure, and that the instinctive reaction to wrench it free was wrong, but her mind recoiled from the thought of the young man having to travel back to the Bay in such agony.

'Nick has sedated him—he can't feel it,' Alex told her, moving aside so that the man could be lifted on to the stretcher.

'Keep his knees up to relieve pressure on his abdomen,' Nick told his helpers.

Leonie repeated Allysha's message, and Alex took her hand in a comforting clasp.

'We would cause more damage if we tried to remove it,' he said, as if he understood her dismay. 'We've got an airway in place and a drip started, but he's haemorrhaging badly and who knows what internal damage has been done?'

'Should one of us go with him in case Nick needs help?' Leonie asked, watching as Nick adjusted the straps on the stretcher so they would secure his patient without affecting the impaled object.

'I suggested that, but he says he'll manage. I think he thinks we might be needed here. I will go to the airport and bring back the other car. I'll see you soon.'

He bent and kissed her lightly on the lips and she noticed the concern in his eyes and little lines of tiredness drawn down his tanned cheeks. She felt a wave of guilt that he was being drawn into her work when he should be enjoying himself.

But would he enjoy himself if he was standing aside when his help or expertise might be needed? She didn't think so! His coming to Australia to pursue the possibilities of finding an inoculation against Murray Valley Encephalitis was proof he liked to be involved—to follow things through. It was another facet of the man she had labelled in her mind as 'a businessman'.

She made her way back through the sand on the track, glad she hadn't pulled on stockings to complete her fine outfit! She'd be able to shake the sand out of her shoes, but getting it out of stockings. . .!

Leonie had done her duty, presenting prizes, and watched another race before Alex returned. He clasped her fingers lightly as he sat down beside her then, as the loudspeaker began an announcement, the pressure tightened.

'The weather bureau advises that the winds predicted for tomorrow are picking up strength and dust in the inland. It is quite probable that we will be caught in a dust storm tomorrow. The organisers have no wish to endanger any-one and would like to point out that our medical facilities are limited. Most pilots are opting to move their planes north or east to avoid the storm. Other visitors must decide whether they wish to leave now or sit out the storm in Talgoola.'

'Your plane?' Leonie asked him.

'It is leaving now. My pilot was at the airport. He had told Allysha he would wait for the four o'clock forecast before he decided, but he knew it was a probability that he would have to go.' He smiled at her. 'Jet engines are expensive things to strip down, clean and rebuild!'

She looked at him, seeing a handsome, successful, sexy, fascinating man she barely knew—and wondered. . .

'You could have gone,' she said, so uncertain that her heartbeat faltered.

'And left you here alone to handle who knows what emergency?'

His eyes were dark, masking all expression, which did nothing to regulate her pulse.

'That's different—I'm on duty,' she said lightly. 'I'm here to stand in for the doctor if he has to take a patient back to town. And I'm not alone. I've the ambulance man and the Army in support, a hospital three hours' drive down the road and a phone to contact the Base if I need a plane flown out here during the night.'

'You'd rather I'd gone?' he asked, and Leonie felt as if she was floundering—drowning in a sea of doubts and questions. She looked around, trying to decide if the announcement had started an exodus. She thought not for people still milled up and down the stairs, and the trumpet rallied the horses for the last race of the day.

'I'm glad you're here,' she told him slowly, trying to frame her thoughts with words, 'because I feel more confident of handling whatever might happen with you, as a doctor, by my side. Yet it embarrasses me because I feel I'm taking advantage of your good nature, or our attraction, or whatever it is between us, and I don't know. . .'

She couldn't continue, turning away from those watchful eyes to see the horses break from the gates.

'Do you think I will demand payment of some kind? Take advantage of the fact that we will be alone tonight?'

She knew she must be scarlet with embarrassment, but she turned back to face him, wanting honesty between them.

'I'd like to say that's worrying me,' she told him, 'but it wouldn't be true. My heart performed its own backflips when it realised we might have the tent to ourselves tonight. You must know I feel this attraction as strongly as you do, but I've the children to consider. I haven't ever had a—'

'Lover?' His voice was politely interested, but she heard an underlying emotion that thrilled in her bones.

'Male friend!' she said firmly, to hide the reaction. 'They think of me as Mum—someone—'

'With no needs of her own? That is selfish of them, surely?'

'They're teenagers, Alex. Selfishness—or self-involvement, self-concern—comes with the package. But it isn't their fault. I brought them up, after all, and now I don't know how to handle this—or even if there's anything to handle. . .'

The uncertainty that bedevilled her whenever she tried to think rationally about Alex choked off her words. She turned to him, wishing he could wave a magic wand and remove all the impediments she saw between them.

Did he see that hopeless plea in her eyes? He looked at her for a silent moment, then raised her hand, turned it palm upwards and pressed a kiss into the centre of it. With a deliberate slowness he closed her fingers, one by one, over the kiss, then slid the closed fist back into her lap.

'You must decide what is best for you, of course, but you must also consider that Mitchell and Caroline are no longer children, and they would be most upset if they thought you considered them that way.'

Not quite a magic wand!

'They're hardly adults,' she argued, while her fingers tried to hold the impression his lips had left on her palm and her mind searched for answers.

'No, they are teenagers, and therefore especially vulnerable, so they must be considered,' he agreed. 'But you have already put your life on hold for a long time. Was that for the children?'

She turned away from eyes that saw too much, looking towards the track but seeing the emptiness of the last twelve years. Could she use the children as an excuse for her non-involvement with anyone else? She shook her head in silent denial, knowing it wasn't true. Non-involvement had been a conscious decision she'd taken, way back then, partly to protect them all. And not getting involved meant not getting hurt and, for those first few years, all she had wanted to do was avoid pain.

She turned back to Alex, knowing she wanted honesty between them.

'I think it became a habit,' she admitted, 'but whatever my reasons were back then it doesn't alter the fact that it happened or make me less anxious about their reactions now.'

He leaned forward and once again he brushed his fingers across her forehead, as if to soothe away her concern. There were probably three thousand people in Talgoola that day, but Leonie was only aware of one man. His eyes met hers, alight with gentle mockery in his solemn face.

'You've never mentioned my phone calls?'

She squirmed in her seat—surely adolescent embarrassment had never been this bad!

'I've told them you rang—mentioned it in passing—but they wouldn't have thought any more of that than they would of Jack phoning me. I'm not a sexual being, remember,' she said, then sighed, for the lightest of touches from this man gave lie to that supposition. 'And you were so far away—more a dream than a reality—what could I say to them?'

She pressed her hands against the feverish heat in her cheeks, and peered at him over her fingertips. Taking a deep breath, she blurted out her other thought—the one that had the most appeal to her peace of mind and least to her conscience.

'I suppose I thought that if you did come back we might have a brief affair, then I could settle back down into my life and they needn't know.'

She glimpsed a glow of anger in the dark eyes, but it was suppressed so quickly that she wondered if she had imagined it.

'And have you considered me in any of these arguments you hold inside that lovely head of yours?'

Shock and embarrassment fought for ascendancy.

'I have! Of course!' she muttered, her eyes repeating her silent pleas for understanding. More heat coursed through her, more confusion! 'But I thought. . .'

He waited, the stand now emptied of its crowds, the sudden silence overwhelming.

'I thought that would be all you wanted, too,' she said, shrugging as if the movement could push away her embarrassment. 'You're a man of the world, but not of my world. . .'

His eyes darkened, but he didn't speak. Instead, he drew her close and kissed her, liberating the demons and flooding her body with so much desire her mind forgot its arguments.

'Sweep 'em out with the trash?' a loud voice cried.

'Better not, she's one of the Flying Doctors mob!' another answered.

Alex released her, and she pushed herself unsteadily away from him and sat back in her seat. Now humiliation was added to embarrassment, she thought, but Alex had turned towards the two cleaners, and she heard him explain with a humorous dignity, 'I've come a long way to kiss this woman, but the crowds and the injured jockey—what with one thing or another, we've barely had a moment's peace.'

The men chuckled, and one said, 'Well, you go to it, mate! Don't let us stop you!'

'No, no, we're in your way. We'll head back to our tent, where the Army first-aid fellows will chaperon us.'

He reached out his hand and helped Leonie to her feet. Impressed by his unflustered handling of the situation, she let herself be helped up and ushered down the steps and away from the stand.

Was it his control that drew her to him? Control over silly situations like that, or life-threatening situations like the one in the restaurant—control over his emotions, his life?

She admired control because she'd tried to achieve it in her own life—and had, until recently, thought she'd succeeded.

Alex led her to the car and helped her in, then climbed behind the wheel and turned to smile at her.

'Back to the tent, or another quick tour of the grounds?'

She returned the smile, but knew he would guess it was

a cover-up! Nothing was settled between them—in fact, the churning uncertainty had worsened.

'Back to the tent. There's a big dinner tonight in the marquee on the far side of the pub. With any luck, we'll have time to shower and change before we have to show up in the official party again.'

'And this is a holiday for you?' he asked in mock horror.

Leonie smiled again, a more genuine effort this time as she felt the tension between them begin to ease.

'The dinner and the dance after it are major fund-raising functions,' she explained. 'It's a case of duty calls.'

'And I had visions of Ascot, and luxury cars—picnics packed in wicker baskets, and soft green grass!'

She was chuckling quietly as they drew up at the tent. She liked his humour, too, and the fact that he could make her feel. . .cared about, protected!

He touched her lightly on the arm. Not to mention incredibly excited! she added silently.

CHAPTER FOUR

'ANOTHER patient, by the look of things.'

Fighting off the demons, she looked towards the tent and saw the two soldiers helping a young man into a chair.

'You don't have to do this, you know,' she said to Alex's back as she hurried after him towards the patient.

He turned and smiled.

'Don't spoil my fun!' he said. 'I try to do volunteer work in a Third World country for a few weeks each year to keep my skills from going rusty. This is like a. . .' his smile widened, lighting up his eyes '. . .a picnic, compared to that!'

Unable to argue, she followed him. He was stripping away the layers of his outer character, revealing an admirable and exciting man. She didn't need that kind of revelation! Much easier to think of him as a cardboard cut-out of a suave businessman. You couldn't fall in love with cardboard cut-outs.

The patient was holding his forearm across his chest, and his face was a chalky white, suggesting acute pain. Alex bent over him, and she could see his fingers feeling around the shoulder joint.

'How did it happen?' he asked the young man, who fidgeted a bit before he answered.

'We were practising ju-jitsu,' he muttered.

'Ah, martial arts! You are an exponent?' Alex straightened up. He frowned, and seemed to be studying the outward conformation of the joint and upper arm.

No,' the fellow confessed. 'It was more fooling around. I had my arm out to one side. I'd just tried a bit of a kick, and my mate kicked at me and hit my biceps. I felt something give and this terrible pain.'

'It's a shoulder dislocation,' Alex said, stepping aside to draw Leonie closer. 'See how the upper arm has this hollow shape compared to his good arm. That is the easiest way to tell without X-rays.'

'I helped reduce dislocations many years ago, but. . . Perhaps we should send him to town in the ambulance.'

'It would be a long painful journey, and I think the fellow would prefer to stay here.' He turned back to his patient. 'Wouldn't you?'

The man nodded, and Alex continued. 'We will try the simple way of slipping it back into place. It will hurt, but only for a moment, and—although it sounds impossible—it will hurt less if you can relax your body. Leonie and one of these soldiers will hold your upper arm against your body, while I rotate your forearm outwards like this.'

He had motioned to his helpers earlier, so Leonie and the first-aid man took their places as he spoke. To the patient it must have seemed as if Alex was demonstrating what he was about to do so he hadn't tensed to wait for possible pain. Then they heard the click, and the young man's relieved sigh.

'Once a shoulder has been dislocated it can happen more easily again. You will have to be careful now because the torn ligaments will be sore for a few days, and careful in the future to avoid it happening again. Sit for a moment. I will find a sling, and some ice to help reduce the pain and swelling.'

He touched Leonie's hand as he walked away, and she recognised it as a signal and followed him.

'I would like him to stay here,' he said when they were out of earshot of the patient. 'It is clear he has had a few drinks, and if he goes back to his companions there is a risk he could begin drinking again. A fall against that arm could seriously damage the joint. What is the procedure?'

'We can suggest he stays,' Leonie told him. 'That's why we have the beds. His shoulder must still be painful. You could hook up fluids and feed him painkillers and a mild sedative through a drip. He might feel more of a patient that way.'

'That's a good idea,' he told her. 'The fluid will help flush the alcohol out of his system and replenish his electrolytes. It will stave off any possibility of delayed shock.'

They walked back outside, and Alex made the suggestion. Leonie saw the relief on the young man's face and realised that he must be feeling shaky to accede so readily. Alex fitted a sling to immobilise his arm, then she led the patient inside.

'Lie down. While Dr Solano organises pain relief for you, I'll take your details. This might look like a roughly painted tent but it is, in fact, a hospital and we need the paperwork done!'

He smiled at her weak joke, but gave his name as Robert Stewart and a Brisbane address. She went through the list of possible allergies, crossing off each as he shook his head. Alex crossed to the bed, a bag of fluid in his hand, and asked the same questions.

'Do you have a drip-stand?' he asked Leonie, and she left him with the patient while she found the portable stand and the other equipment he would need.

Robert's friends arrived and were sent back to their camp to get his backpack, while the soldiers were replaced by a solitary sentry. He came into the tent to introduce himself and announce that he was on duty while the medical staff went to dinner.

'Have many people left to avoid the dust storm?' Leonie asked him.

'Not enough!' he said gloomily. 'I reckon we've got well over a thousand still here, although some might go after dinner tonight. Could be chaotic tomorrow.'

'You sound as if you know about dust storms,' Alex remarked.

'Had one in the Northern Territory once when I was on manoeuvres,' he explained. 'It's OK as long as you're prepared to sit it out, close your tent or caravan and stay put until it passes over. It's when people panic that things go wrong. I guess you fellows know that.'

Leonie smiled at being one of 'you fellows' but she knew the lugubrious soldier was right. Dust storms were a nuisance because of the massive clean-up needed afterwards, but panic could be a killer.

'Well, I'm going to have a quick shower before dinner,' she announced, not wanting to add to the gloomy predictions. She turned to Alex.

'You know the way?'

'To your shower or mine?' he teased, so softly that only she could hear.

Her heart bounded in response and her body ached to be held against his—to feel his arms around her and his lips demanding the passion she hadn't known she could feel.

'Bearing in mind we're supposed to be at the dinner in

fifteen minutes, I think yours,' she said reluctantly, but as she gathered up clean clothes she wondered how a word, or look, or touch could excite her so much that she could forget all her doubts and uncertainties. Forget her children! Forget the past! And wish to live only for the moment—for the day!

She was still questioning her reactions to Alex when she returned to the tent, aware that her deceptively simple black dress could be described as sexy! It hung demurely from ties on her shoulders, simple and unadorned, but the silk clung to her body as she moved, whispering against her skin and suggesting, rather than exposing, the feminine shape beneath it.

'So, with a new room-mate in the tent you feel it's safe to tantalise me?' he asked, standing back to admire her—his eyes revealing his approval.

'You don't look so bad yourself,' she replied, wondering if Nick or Jack had mentioned that many of the male guests would wear formal evening wear.

Not so bad! her heart echoed. He looked as if his body had been moulded into his clothes—as if he'd been born in a dinner suit! And the crisp white shirt and fine black wool only enhanced his distinguished good looks.

'So, we will leave you in charge,' he said to their new 'sentry'. 'We will not be far away if you need us.'

He put out his arm, and Leonie slipped her hand into the fold of his elbow, her demons breaking free of the nominal restraints she'd tried to place on them and dancing through her body.

The dinner began quietly, with the chairman of the organising committee repeating the news that the winds were growing stronger and that the dust storm had become a probability instead of a possibility.

'It is expected to reach Talgoola in the early hours of the morning and should clear by lunchtime, but all of you know how reliable weather forecasting is.'

A burst of laughter greeted this remark, but the party sobered again when he repeated his warning that there was still time to leave.

'The storm is moving east along a two-hundred-kilometre front so a couple of hours' drive north or south will take you out of it. For those of you travelling east, if you leave later this evening you should stay in front of it or at least reach Hopewell and proper shelter before it strikes. If you wish to stay on we would advise you remain inside your shelter until the storm has passed over. The Army has emergency tents for those who had intended sleeping under the stars.'

His warnings were greeted by subdued conversation but, looking around at the unconcerned faces of the merry-makers, Leonie doubted whether many more would depart.

'If the storm is past by midday, will tomorrow's races take place?' Alex asked.

A guest across the table replied, 'Of course, they will. A little dust won't hurt the horses. In fact, it might make the track softer.'

Leonie smiled as Alex studied the woman's tanned and weather-lined face, obviously puzzling over whether she was joking or not.

He shook his head and laughed, a deep, rich sound that raced through Leonie's blood.

'The chairman stands up and calmly suggests we finish dinner then, if we want to leave, drive north or south a few hours to escape the dust—and you tell me the races will go on.'

'I'm Mavis Crooke,' the woman across the table said. 'My grandparents settled in these parts nearly one hundred years ago. Back then it took a week to reach Hopewell, and it was the size Talgoola is today! But when the prime minister of the day visited Hopewell the whole family went in to greet him, although it'd been raining for weeks and they had to swim the horses across three rivers on the way. A little dust stop the races? Phooey, young man!'

She turned from Alex in mock disgust and Leonie chuckled.

'Young man!' she teased, then caught her breath as he turned, smiling, towards her.

'See how you strip the age from me,' he murmured. 'Didn't I tell you how you made me feel?'

Her heart jolted irregularly, and she battled to make sense of this situation. A brief courtship when she was nineteen, two babies by the time she was twenty-three, a disastrous end to her marriage and then—nothing! What experience did she have to judge this man against? Was this normal flirtation between two people who were attracted to each other or something more than that? And what would come of it? What could come of it?

Nothing! she reminded herself, but the nagging questions kept her silent through dinner. Until Alex took her in his arms to dance with her on the tiny dance-floor set up at one end of the marquee, and she remembered she had some responsibility to him as a guest.

'Do you think. . .?' Leonie looked up to ask him a question but the look in his eyes stole away her words.

'So calm, your eyes,' he murmured, 'like tranquil lakes

in a silvery dawn. Do you know why you intrigue me?'

She shook her head, bound in a spell he was weaving about her.

He drew her closer but held her gaze, and his lips sent a silent kiss her way.

'Because of the fires beneath that tranquillity—because those lovely eyes mask the passion you have frozen into quiescence deep inside you. Your cool composure issues a challenge, Leonie, an invitation to any red-blooded man to plunge into those icy waters and find the fire beneath them!'

Her mind split apart, the rational part of her brain relieved. A challenge was something she could understand. It explained his interest in her very nicely. Better yet, it reinforced her belief that, for all his talk, an affair was all he wanted. Once the challenge was accepted and won—and he would win, she knew that—he would return to Europe, and her life would return to normal.

But for all her brave words about there being no future for them—in spite of all her reasoned arguments, in spite of knowing it was impossible—the sensory heart of her mind screamed in silent pain, aching to be a loved one, not a challenge—for this interlude to be a beginning, not an end in itself!

They were still dancing in silence at ten o'clock when the chairman called for silence, and stood up to present the special guests and representatives of the organisations who would benefit from the festivities.

Leonie walked up to the podium, acknowledging the applause she knew was for the Service—not for herself—and briefly quoted figures.

'Most of you know that the RFDS covers more than

seven million square kilometres of our continent. Australia-wide, we provide service to more than three thousand patients each week and carry out fifteen thousand emergency evacuations a year. Here in Queensland, our area, the demand for service has expanded, with new planes based in Brisbane and Rockhampton.

'The battle to keep up with the costs of these services is never-ending, and it is only through the generosity of people like those on this committee—and you who attend these functions—that the Royal Flying Doctor Service can continue to spread its mantle of safety across the isolated parts of our great country.'

She smiled her thanks at the applause, and stepped down from the rostrum.

'Those figures are true?' Alex demanded as she rejoined him at their table.

She was surprised by the question, but not surprised by the sudden switch from lover to businessman.

'They were Australian figures, not Rainbow Bay figures,' she hastened to assure him. 'You've only seen the operation of one base.'

He frowned, considering this, then insisted that she list the other bases and the areas they covered.

'What a great man, your John Flynn, who started all of this,' he murmured. 'To have had the vision to foresee the difference that air transport could make—not now, when we all take planes for granted, but back then, at a time when planes were still experimental.'

Leonie felt a thrill of pride and pleasure. He must have read the book she'd sent him on the founder of the RFDS, and the tone of his voice told her how much he admired the work they were doing.

The band struck up again, but they didn't dance. Mavis had returned to the table and was telling Alex wild tales of the pioneering days. Leonie had a quiet talk to a nurse from Hopewell who had worked with the Service many years ago, then the chairman relayed the latest weather bureau warning and the party broke up.

But if the atmosphere in the marquee had been more subdued than in previous years the noise from the camping ground told them that the impending storm was doing little to dampen the spirits of the younger revellers.

'Do we attempt to sleep through that?' Alex asked.

'You're a doctor,' Leonie reminded him. 'Didn't your training include learning to sleep whenever and wherever you got the chance? It was one of the essentials of survival for nurses!'

He drew her close and kissed her temple.

'When I'm tired I can sleep anywhere,' he murmured, 'even alone in a narrow camp bed!' He paused and his teeth nibbled at her ear.

'When I'm tired!' he repeated softly, steering her away from the tent and out towards their 'ambulance', parked in the shadows beneath a windmill.

'Let's star-gaze for a while and talk of you and me,' he suggested, helping her into the front seat, then walking around to sit behind the wheel. He took her hand and traced patterns in her palm, the sharp impression of his fingernails sending tremors along her nerves.

'It's impossible,' she said, more to herself than to him, as she shut away the image of the whole man and her own insidious dreams of for ever. 'We're as far apart as the earth is from those stars. Our lives have touched; let's take what pleasure we can from the coincidence.'

'And if I want more than that?' he asked, his voice rumbling with what could be anger—or desire.

She shrugged.

'More than an affair? What more could there be between us?'

'This?' he murmured, and drew her closer, somehow managing to make her feel comfortable in the awkward contours of the bucket seats. His lips pressed against her shoulder and she fought the demons, denying the inner music that had set their feet tapping. She felt the loose silk tie give way and his lips travel lower, nibbling at her skin—his tongue stroking the edge of lace that defined her aching, swelling breast.

'I won't deny I want you,' she told him, furious at her body's response, 'but one day you'll be gone. You've said yourself it's a challenge! And I can cope with that. What I can't handle is the damage it could do to my relationship with my children.' She paused, uncertain how he would react. 'I'd rather they didn't know!'

'And have you also decided where we should conduct this oh-so-secret affair?' he growled, his lips returning to torment the sensitive skin beneath her ear.

Heat flooded her body. Did he think she had actually planned it all?

'Don't be ridiculous,' she faltered. 'I haven't thought of it at all, except. . .'

In dreams, she wanted to say, only in the dreams that it didn't have to end, which was why dreams were so satisfactory.

'Except?'

Now his lips were pressed against her nape, producing a shivery sensation of total bliss.

'It's impossible!' she muttered, fighting the weakness in her bones and the heat between her thighs. 'The whole thing's a nonsense. I should have sent the flowers back and hung up on your calls!'

'Impossible?'

The tantalising lips had breathed the word against her skin, damp yet so hot that she could feel it branded into her skin.

'Impossible!' she repeated, fighting a desperate rear-guard action against his sexual mastery. 'You're a jet-setter, a man with homes in Italy and Switzerland, apartments in New York and London—but not at Rainbow Bay, where I belong, where—'

His lips moved to smother the words, and she forgot her argument as the waves of desire rose higher, swamping her brain cells, destroying reason and leaving only sensation.

What seemed like an aeon later he released her, and she sank back weakly into the bucket seat and tilted her head back to gulp at the cool night air.

'The stars are gone!'

It was an idle observation, but hearing the words made her realise their significance.

'The dust! It's already moving across the camp.'

She forced her lethargic body into action, leaping from the vehicle and racing across towards the tent. Their patient was asleep and the soldier was lying on another camp-bed, reading a thick paperback novel.

'I want to repack all this equipment,' she told Alex, who had followed her into the tent and was checking Robert's pulse.

The soldier sat up. 'Dust coming?' he asked tersely.

She nodded, and he rose to his feet.

'I'll check the guy ropes and close the small tent,' he said.

Leonie pulled out the equipment bags and began to repack them. Alex finished with his patient and joined her, standing so close that she fancied she could hear his heart beating. She pretended to a calm efficiency she was far from feeling and explained what she was doing.

'I've put all the drips and their equipment into this one, the drugs are still in their locked case and I'm stacking masks, antihistamines, bronchodilator drugs and epinephrine into this one. Oxygen bottles and nebuliser are in that one over there.'

'You're expecting allergic reactions and asthma? Surely anyone with bronchial weakness would have left when they heard the warnings?'

'Common sense is not a prerequisite to attend a party like those campers are having,' she pointed out, hearing the sounds of merriment still echoing from the campgrounds. She could have added that it was in short supply inside the tent, but every time she'd tried to talk to him she'd tangled her feet in her sentences and tripped herself up on her words!

She pushed the clean linen into a large plastic bag and tied it closed. Alex's presence was having a strange effect on her nerve endings and her skin was prickling uncomfortably.

'I've rigged up a light outside so people will know we're here, but we should keep the door zipped closed,' the soldier called.

'I'll go across to the bathroom first,' Leonie replied, digging through her clothes for a T-shirt and cotton shorts.

If she was called out in the night at least she'd be respectable.

'I've put our overnight bags into a plastic bag,' Alex told her when she returned. She looked at him as he spoke, and realised that he'd also had a shower and changed into a knitted shirt and shorts. His dark hair, shot with silver lights, gleamed wetly and tiny droplets of water nested in the silky dark hairs on his forearms.

She fought the impulse to reach out and brush them away, knowing that to touch him would unleash her demons once again.

'Patient!'

The call came a fraction of a second before she said to hell with the demons. She hurried around the meagre partition which provided a modicum of privacy to the back to the tent and heard the tortured breathing of the young girl immediately.

The soldier had settled her in a chair, and Leonie went immediately to their 'respiration' case, asking questions as she collected the equipment she would need.

'Are you asthmatic?' She plugged the nebuliser into the lead, and fitted an adult size mask to it.

The girl nodded in reply.

'Have you taken anything now?'

Her patient waved a familiar Ventolin puffer at her, her wheezing so bad that Leonie could imagine the constriction of the tiny tubes in the girl's lungs which had reacted so quickly to the irritation of the dust.

'Allergic to any drugs?' A quick headshake of denial.

Alex was beside her now, and held the cup of the nebuliser while she broke open an ampoule of bronchodilator and emptied it into the plastic container. Their fingers touched as he took control and screwed the mask into place. Leonie ignored her physical reaction and crossed to the girl, helping her fit the mask across her mouth and nose.

As she turned on the power she saw the white vapour swirl and left the patient on her own while she found an oximeter. Attached to the girl's forefinger, it would indicate the oxygen level in her blood. Once this had been fitted Leonie picked up a file and wrote down what she had done.

'Do you use steroids as well as your inhalant? Prednisolone, or something similar?'

Alex asked the question but again the girl shook her head.

'We've got prednisolone in the case,' Leonie told him quietly, 'but it often takes longer to work. Do you think four-hourly on the nebuliser will be as effective?'

'Not only as effective, but a good excuse to keep her here.'

Something in his voice made her look up into his face.

'A good excuse?'

He grinned at her.

'I'm counting the beds. How many more patients before we have to share?'

The words whispered across her skin, and her fingers shook on the file she was clutching.

'Go to bed!' she hissed at him. 'I can manage this patient, but if something more alarming turns up you might not have the opportunity to sleep later.'

His smile widened, revealing a glimpse of white teeth.

'Sleep?' he echoed. 'Sleep was the furthest thing from my mind!'

She gasped at her body's reaction, but fought on doggedly.

'With all these people sharing our tent, sleep is all you'll be doing,' she muttered furiously. 'Now, got to bed and let me get this poor kid settled for the night.'

He leaned closer and his lips brushed against her cheek.

'It wasn't me who suggested we have an affair,' he murmured, tiny lights like golden devils dancing in his dark eyes. 'But, having given the idea some serious consideration, I find it has an infinite appeal.'

She battled for air. It was the husky tone as much as the words that had filled her with longing again, yet disappointment drifted like cobwebs across the excitement. Had she wanted him to argue more vehemently against an affair? To deny that that was his intention?

He moved away but she could see his shadow on the material that formed the partition, strangely elongated—like a spirit from another world enticing her onwards.

Definitely from another world, she reminded herself tartly, returning to her new patient as the last drops of medication spluttered in the nebuliser. She turned it off and took the mask from the girl.

'Are you willing to stay the night?' she asked. 'You should have another dose before morning.'

'I'd love to stay,' the girl said gratefully. 'This attack came on suddenly, and my friends had no idea I needed help. Fortunately, we're camped near the showers, and one of the soldiers brought me over on a little motorbike.'

Leonie led her to a bed, then took her name and address: Angie Webster, with a home address in Adelaide.

'I've been working my way around Australia,' she explained. 'At the moment I'm waitressing at the resort on Turtle Island—out from Rainbow Bay.'

Turtle Island! Remote, and exclusive—but hardly the kind of place Mitchell had been thinking of when he'd suggested that she take a 'proper holiday.'

So why was she feeling pathetically excited? Because Alex had asked where they might go?

She concentrated on completing what she could of the file, checked the monitor, noting that Angie's oxygen level in her blood had improved, then cleaned out the cup of the nebuliser and placed it and another ampoule ready for the next medication. She tucked a plastic bag around the machine and draped a towel over it. The flapping of the tent walls told her that the wind was picking up, and she could taste the dust already filtering into the tent.

Surgical masks! Which bag had masks? She forced herself to think, not wanting to expose equipment unnecessarily. She closed her eyes and pictured the contents of equipment cases she'd packed and repacked so often as part of her job.

They were under the dressings! She knelt down and pulled out the bag she needed, opening it and searching through it for the masks. Once found, she snapped the locks shut on the case and slid the masks into a plastic bag. She'd leave them on the table where they could reach them easily.

'You get some sleep; I'll call you if you're needed,' the soldier whispered.

'Or in three and a half hours if I don't wake up. I need to check on Angie.'

He waved her away and, after a last glance at her patients, she headed towards the back section of the tent.

Was Alex asleep? He lay so still yet, as she settled onto

her own narrow bed, she was as aware of him as if he lay beside her. Was it possible to send waves of awareness through the air? Could he be doing it deliberately that she could feel his lips feather up her spine, his fingers slide across her breasts?

She shivered and tried to curl her knees up close to her chest to protect her body from the invasive waves of sensuality. But the bed was too narrow, and he was too close.

CHAPTER FIVE

LEONIE woke to the sound of voices and sat up, rubbing her eyes and feeling the dusty deposits left while she'd slept. The tent was dark, but a shaded light glowed beyond the partition. The canvas flapped in a strengthened wind and she could hear a sound like sandpaper scraping across the fabric. It was the dust, she realised, flung against the thin walls of the tent with an unrelenting fury.

Running her fingers through her hair, she slipped quietly out of bed, but Alex was already up—bent over a patient on the stretcher in the middle of the room. Leonie moved silently, yet he must have sensed her coming, for he turned and his quick smile set up a chain reaction through her veins.

'He's complaining of bad stomach cramps, diarrhoea and vomiting,' he explained in a whisper, while his hands pressed against the man's abdomen.

No mention of the storm beyond their haven—but if he could take it all for granted so could she!

'Food poisoning?' she suggested, praying that she was wrong. The common bacteria that proliferated in food would love the conditions at Talgoola, especially the inadequate refrigeration.

Alex finished his examination, held a bowl while the man was sick again and then suggested that he shift into one of the camp-beds—the last 'hospital' bed they had, apart from the soldier's. As the patient made his way over to the bed Alex drew Leonie aside.

'I gave him an electrolyte replacement drink but, as you saw, his stomach won't tolerate the liquid. What would your normal procedure be?'

'Is he badly dehydrated?' she asked.

'Sufficiently so to cause concern.'

She smiled at the formal pronouncement, suspecting that he was enjoying 'playing doctor'.

'Then we'd maybe drip fluid into him,' she suggested.

'And drugs? Antiemetics for the vomiting or opiates for the diarrhoea?'

She shook her head, and smiled again.

'I'm a nurse, remember! We try everything else first! And, although I might be a bit out of touch, I'm certain the RFDS protocol is to avoid drugs in cases where we suspect salmonella poisoning because of the suspicion that they can prolong the illness or cause colon problems.'

'So you reject my drugs, although making them is my livelihood,' he teased.

'Don't you also make antisecretory preparations? We use those for persistent diarrhoea, pepto-bismuth, I'll get some and some fluid.'

She crossed to the equipment boxes, pulling the fluid case out from underneath the plastic cover. Dust made the surfaces gritty, and her fingers felt clumsy as she fitted the tubes to the soft bag. Alex had found a drip-stand and set it up beside the patient. Leonie closed her eyes for a moment, praying that the man wasn't the first of many.

Above them the wind howled its anguish. Every now and then a stronger gust would lift a tent peg and their walls would sag, then settle back again. Pretending to a calm she didn't feel, she checked their other patients, but her mind was racing as she thought ahead. A salmonella outbreak in the middle of a dust storm! Could anything be worse?

Ocular allergy! She was bathing a pair of incredibly inflamed eyes, six hours and no sleep later, when she realised this! Her own eyes ached and the corneas felt scratched by the dust she was constantly blinking out of them, but they weren't swollen almost shut.

'Will they be all right?' her patient, a young woman, asked.

'They'll be fine, but do try not to rub them. And keep out of the wind. You can stay here but I can't offer you a bed. There's sitting room only out the back there.'

She gestured towards the rear of the tent where many of their patients were sitting on the camp-beds, the more lively of them playing a quiet game of cards. She suspected that those with eye problems were too disorientated to want to go outside, and the gastro patients liked the proximity to the hotel facilities.

'I'll give you some antihistamine tablets to take. Don't drink with them, and don't drive because they could make you sleepy.'

'Drive?' the woman said. 'Have you been outside lately? The dust's so thick you couldn't see from one side of the road to the other.'

Leonie *had* been outside, but only to hurry with head bent and shoulders hunched against the wind to the hotel, shepherding patients to the toilet. They had five now, including three children, with food poisoning. The Army had provided more emergency beds and the ambulance had taken another two children and their mothers to

Hopewell. She knew the second ambulance was on its way, but the dust was still too thick for planes to fly safely into the town.

She had spent the hours since four in the morning, when the voices had woken her, tending to the people who had begun to stream in for help as the dust grew thicker and the elusive gastroenteritis bug spread through the tent community. From time to time she'd heard loudspeakers adjuring people to remain under cover, and knew the Army personnel must be patrolling outside. But there'd been no rest inside their tent, no time to walk outside even if she'd wanted to leave the sheltering canvas.

Angie was still wheezing but had graduated to a chair, allowing someone else to have her bed. Robert sat beside her, talking quietly. Leonie realised that his company was as good as a drug for the girl, and his continued presence in the hospital tent meant that he was keeping off alcohol and protecting his shoulder.

And Alex, on whom the major burden of the disaster had fallen, was happily 'playing doctor'.

New patients continued to present themselves, clutching at their cramping stomachs, holding handkerchiefs over aching sinuses or with eyes red and swollen. The dust must be carrying some pollens from inland, and the irritant was inflaming eyes and affecting sinuses nearly as successfully as the suspected salmonella was infecting intestines.

'Antihistamine!' Alex's voice made her spin around. She excused herself and hurried over to the drug case.

'We're running out,' she said, peering in at the depleted stocks. 'There should be some in the emergency packs, and the first-aid fellows might carry it.'

She handed him a card of tablets, and felt his fingers close on hers.

'We'll manage,' he said so reassuringly that she wanted to cry. She looked up at this man who'd erupted back into her life less than forty-eight hours ago. He was covered in a layer of the fine reddish dust that had infiltrated every corner of the tent, and when he smiled it left deep indentations in his cheeks. She wanted to say how grateful she was for his help, but didn't know where to begin.

Pulling her hand away, she turned to open the emergency packs to seek the antihistamines. She'd stopped keeping accurate track of medications two hours ago. The requisitions for new supplies were going to be a nightmare!

'Found some? Great work!' Alex was so cheerful, so lavish with his praise for the most minor of assistance, that she felt ashamed of her own irritation with the situation.

'Not quite the weekend you'd envisaged?' she said quietly, as much to keep him talking as for any other reason.

'The weekend's not over yet!' he reminded her, his deep voice heavy with meaning and the message in his dark eyes lighting fires in the innermost part of her being.

'I'd better speak to the first-aid fellows about their drugs!' she said nervously. She was flustered by her reaction. All thoughts of pleasure had vanished when patients had begun crowding into their tent. She had been on her feet for hours, stopping only for a hurried breakfast brought over from the hotel about a lifetime ago. And Alex had been working harder than she had. He should be exhausted, not thinking of. . .sex?

She unzipped the tent flap and hurried over to the hotel. The Army's first-aid team had set up their own surgery, and were only referring the worst of their patients on to the tent.

'Do you fellows carry antihistamine?' she asked. 'We're running out.'

'We're short ourselves,' the senior soldier told her, 'but the ambulance is bringing fresh supplies. I heard your doctor mate on the phone to the hospital earlier. He gave them quite a list.'

So Alex had saved the day again! She didn't know if she felt relieved or annoyed. Her cardboard cut-out had been knocked flat by the kind, unflappable human being she'd worked with all morning, and now he'd proved himself a better organiser than she was.

And she prided herself on her organisational skills!

'Dust or no dust, I'm going to have a shower and change into clean clothes,' he announced a little later.

Leonie glanced at her watch.

'It's midday,' she told him. 'The dust is supposed to have gone.'

He put his arm around her shoulders and they walked towards the tent flaps—looking like two beings from outer space with their coating of dust, the white face masks they were both wearing turned red from the ochre colouring.

Outside the dust still swirled in the unearthly light—a late dawn or early dusk! The sun couldn't penetrate the cloud, but the wind had dropped and some of the particles were now drifting downward.

'Will they hold the races?' Alex asked, hunching protectively over her as they looked around at the dirt-shrouded landscape.

'I doubt it,' she said, nodding towards the shadowy outline of the hotel. 'Unless horses' eyes can see through dust, they won't see where they're going.'

He chuckled and hugged her closer then, as a gust whipped up again, he hurried her back inside and zipped the door closed behind them.

'Go and have your shower,' she reminded him. In spite of her tiredness, his arm around her shoulders was causing internal problems, and she needed space—and time apart from him—to settle her demons.

'I'll be right back!' he promised, in the husky voice that set her pulses rioting.

She shook her head, unable to believe the effect he had on her—and disbelieving, as well, that he could still show interest. If the other people in the tent were any indication of how she looked, then her fair hair would be a matted browny-orange colour, her eyes would be rimmed with dust and, now she'd taken off her mask, there must be a white patch on her face that would make her look like an anaemic clown!

She checked each patient once again, and admitted two more food-poisoning cases to her 'hospital'. At some stage she and Alex had conferred and decided to try oral rehydration in all adults, saving the IV fluids they had for children. But they had kept the more seriously affected adults in the tent where they could be monitored, and were using an antiemetic injection if the vomiting persisted.

The children were sleeping, but the other occupants chatted quietly or lay, with their eyes closed, waiting out this siege of nature. Certain that they were all comfortable, Leonie found her overnight bag and dug out fresh clothes.

Her smart black and white suit and the silk dress she'd worn to the dinner were hanging, with a cheery, hot-pink number she'd chosen for today, from one of the central poles in a plastic suit-bag. A rueful smile parted her lips as she compared the dream of these few days with the reality. Fresh underwear, a clean cotton T-shirt and a pair of linen shorts—that was as sexy as she'd be getting today.

She was feeling in the bag for a clean handkerchief when her fingers closed on the tiny bottle of perfume Caroline had spent her entire savings on last Christmas. It wasn't Leonie's usual light and flowery scent, but a dark, exotic mix of fragrances which had made her head reel when she first tried it.

She couldn't remember packing it but, not wanting to lose it, she tucked it into her toiletry bag, gathered up the clean clothes and her towel and was ready to leave when Alex returned.

The clean, fresh scent of him preceded his physical arrival. Was it because of the dust that her senses were more alert, or was she attuned to him in some way?

'It may be worth enduring your outback dust for the special delight of being clean once again,' he announced, coming around the partition and spreading his arms wide for approval. The seated patients applauded, and one made a little speech of gratitude. Only Leonie remained silent, her senses enmeshed in the sight and sound and smell of him. She squatted on the ground beside her bag and tried to steady her nerves.

This couldn't happen, she told herself, but her arousal was as real as it had been when he had touched and kissed her—when his lips had murmured seductively against her skin. Without so much as a glance in her direction, he had overpowered her senses and breached the already shaky walls of her defences.

She stood up carefully, afraid that her feelings might

be visible to everyone in the restricted space behind the partition. A quick glance told her that the card players had returned to their game, and the other patients had resumed their conversations.

She didn't look at Alex, but felt him closing on her until his shadow fell across her shoulder and she could almost taste the still-damp heat emanating from his body.

'Our patients are all quiet,' he murmured, for her ears alone. 'I could come and wash your back for you.'

So, he had seen her reaction!

'I think I'll manage,' she told him, but an image of the two of them, their naked bodies slick with water—slippery—soapy—flesh on flesh—rose up so vividly that her knees began to shake.

She met his eyes, silently pleading to be released from this enthralment.

'It hasn't been much of a weekend for you,' she stammered.

The beautiful lips stretched into a smile, and the fantastic golden lights danced in his dark eyes.

'Oh, but it has been!' he whispered, the words like a caress on her gritty skin. 'It has been most enlightening!'

She must have frowned, for he reached out as he'd done before and smoothed the skin on her forehead.

'Go and shower,' he said, turning her towards the door and giving her a gentle shove in that direction.

She went, outwardly calm but inwardly fleeing forces she could not understand—and probably not control. They were moving towards intimacy with an inevitability that frightened her. Gone were any images of a light-hearted affair—a mutually enjoyable 'interlude' to brighten up her life! This new desire was like a deep, dark, swirling current, a forerunner to a tidal wave of passion which would sweep away all sanity—and leave what wreckage in its wake?

She washed off the dust and shampooed her hair, seeing the water run thick and red. And she tried to wash away the awareness that twitched at her skin and prickled down her spine, but water could only do so much.

She dried her traitorous body, then looked at it critically, trying to see it as a lover might see it.

Full, high breasts, still taut in spite of two breast-fed children, flat stomach and well-rounded hips. They'd always been the bane of her existence, but the flesh was firm and the wide bones gave them their shape.

She peered closer. Creamy white skin unmarked, as yet, by age, and a tuft of silvery fair hair, curling close against her skin, protective of her womanhood.

She felt herself blushing, and saw the pinkness flash across her cheeks. Seizing a small plastic bottle of moisturiser, she began to rub the liquid into her body, easing the tightness the dry, dusty weather had caused.

These fantasies must stop, she told herself, determined to get her mind and body back under control. She pulled on her clean underwear, relishing the feel of the soft fabric against her skin. It was her one personal extravagance, buying these slinky scraps of lace and silk or satin which she wore beneath everything from shorts to her smartly tailored business clothes.

Her T-shirt was from the Outback shop beside the Base, navy blue with the winged emblem of the RFDS embossed across the chest. Navy shorts completed her outfit, and the casually smart effect of her reflection pleased her more than the yearning naked wimp she'd viewed earlier.

Yet, as she reached for moisturiser to use on her face her fingers once again touched the tiny vial and she pulled it out, opened it and dabbed a drop beneath each ear and others in the hollow at the base of her throat, between her breasts and on each wrist.

Too much? She sniffed suspiciously but knew that it wasn't an overpowering perfume that wafted round the wearer like a suffocating cloud. It was a scent that worked on skin temperature, releasing its power in sweet, seductive tones only to those who wore it or who were in contact with the wearer.

She smiled uncertainly at her reflected self, then bundled up her dirty clothes and left the bathroom.

'More trouble,' the soldier on the verandah warned her, waving towards the tent.

The screams issuing from within it would have been warning enough, she thought as she hurried through the lessening dust towards the noise.

A small boy lay on the stretcher they used for examining patients, screaming lustily. His mother was hopping up and down impatiently on the other side and crying volubly, making a duet with the child's noise, while a burly man, presumably the child's father, shouted abuse at a tense and wary Alex.

Leonie took in the situation at a glance, and drew a deep breath.

'This is a hospital tent, not a circus. If the noise doesn't stop immediately I will put you all outside!'

Alex looked more surprised than the rest of them, but the noise level dropped immediately. The boy hiccuped a few times, the woman looked sulky and the man frowned at Leonie, but she had seen Alex's shoulders relax and knew that her outburst had been worthwhile.

'What's happening?' she asked him, speaking quietly to give a lead to the over-excited parents.

'He fell off a ride,' Alex explained. 'Hurt his arm. I suspect it could be a greenstick fracture of the radius or ulna, but with no X-ray—'

'He fell off a ride? Are the rides operating? I thought everyone had been told to stay inside as much as possible. How can we keep people out of the dust if the sideshow noise is calling them outside?'

'We run the ride!' the man announced, a defensive tone in his voice. 'And Joey was bored. All the kids are bored. We turned it on to give them a bit of fun—that's all.'

One quick glance at Alex told Leonie that he shared her frustration.

'Has the ambulance arrived?' she asked.

'Not yet,' he told her. 'It will be a longer trip with the visibility reduced by the dust.'

'Then let's splint and wrap the boy's arm,' she said. She turned to the parents. 'We can give you painkillers for him—some paracetemol—and immobilise it, but that's all we can do. You'll have to take him to town for an X-ray. If it's broken they'll put it in plaster.'

'But we can't go to town today—it costs us heaps to bring our gear all the way out here. If we don't run the rides we don't make money,' the woman complained, confirming Leonie's suspicions. 'Lots of the sideshow people are turning on their rides!'

'And encouraging people out into the dust so they can get all kinds of allergic reactions,' Leonie muttered to herself as she located a child-sized splint and bandages.

'Won't the dust affect your motors?' Alex was asking

the man when she returned with the things he would need.

'We can clean our motors but we can't manufacture money,' the woman snapped, giving the impression that she'd had this argument earlier—and her husband had lost!

The family had departed when the wailing of a siren announced the arrival of the ambulance. The two attendants tumbled into the tent, exhausted by a drive which had taken five hours instead of three. Leonie broke up the card game and sent her mobile patients back to their own shelters, freeing the two beds for the tired men.

'You think the worst is over?' Alex asked, standing beside her as she made tea for them.

'Let's hope so,' she told him, hiding a shiver of reaction as his arm brushed against her shoulder. He reached out to lift the plate of sandwiches supplied by the hotel and she saw him hesitate, move closer and heard the deep intake of his breath.

'More challenge, Leonie?' he growled so softly that only she could hear. 'You dare me with that perfume when our tent is full of patients and the parents of patients?'

The demons shot tiny lances of desire into her skin, and hot tea slopped from the mugs she had lifted as he spoke.

'Caroline gave it to me,' she muttered, putting down the cups and mopping at her wet fingers.

He smiled and shook his head.

'Then not both your children are certain you're asexual,' he murmured, and walked away, leaving her puzzling over the remark.

Thinking didn't help much so she carried tea in to the new arrivals.

'Have they cancelled the races?'

The question brought her mind back to the present and

she looked at the ambulance man who had asked the question.

'I've no idea!' she told him. 'I think I heard a new announcement about an hour ago but I wasn't listening.'

A protesting scream of hastily applied brakes broke into their conversation, and the heightened buzz of conversation from the front of the tent brought her hurrying back to the fray.

A dust-encrusted soldier wiped a weary hand across his face.

'If I get our first-aid bloke to take over here could you two come across to the fairground with us?'

'Of course!' Alex responded, and ushered Leonie towards the door, cutting off the questions she'd been about to ask. Once outside he explained his haste. 'Whatever the trouble, I thought it better not to upset our patients with details.'

I should have thought of that, she realised, wondering if it was tiredness or hormonal confusion dulling her judgement.

Let it be tiredness, her mind prayed. That's more easily cured!

They climbed into the Army Jeep and sped off, the driver explaining on the way that the tall Ferris wheel had become stuck and people were stranded and panicking at the top of its arc.

'But don't they have a manual release which allows it to come slowly down?' Leonie asked, remembering a similar incident at the Rainbow Bay Show years earlier.

'It's not working either,' the soldier said gloomily. 'We told those people not to start the rides. We've had several tonnes of dust dropped on this place in the last ten hours, and they should have known it would affect their motors. Even our trucks, which are built for tough conditions, are packing up.'

He pressed on his horn to make a passage for the vehicle.

'So all the people who stayed on through the storm are now gathered here?' Alex observed.

The wind had dropped but dust hung like a miasma around them as they made their way on foot to the base of the Ferris wheel.

'Two of our fellows are climbing up with ropes,' their guide explained. 'They'll secure the ropes and then lower the people, starting with those making the most noise.'

Hysterical screams from above provided emphasis for his words.

'I'm not up on panic and hysteria,' she whispered to Alex.

He slid one arm around her waist and drew her close.

'I suspect it will cure itself when they reach the ground. I rather think we're here in case a rope breaks or someone clambers out of their seat and plummets to the ground.'

'Oh, great! I'm so glad you pointed that out!' she told him, nearly dizzy with tiredness—or was it desire?

Shouts from above signalled that something was about to happen, then the crowd hushed as a small figure was lifted free of a cradle on the machine and carefully lowered towards the ground.

'Stand back! Make room! Give them air!' one of the soldiers shouted, and the crowd surged obediently backward.

Khaki-clad arms stretched upward to receive the young girl, whose tear-streaked face broke into sunny smiles when she recognised an older sibling and then saw her mother pushing through the crowd towards her, alternately crying and scolding as relief gave way to anger.

The rope with its special safety harness swung upwards again and then down with a teenager, the source of the hysterics. Dangling on the end of a rope must have frozen her vocal chords for her descent was made in silence. She reached the ground, gave one final scream and crumpled into a quiet heap at the feet of the soldiers supervising the rescue.

'It's only a faint—tip her head forward between her knees,' Alex said, as Leonie knelt beside the girl and felt for a pulse.

She was already stirring when they eased her head forward, and a minute later had shrugged their helping hands away and was looking around in confusion.

Leonie saw her pupils dilate and her lips begin to open.

'You're perfectly all right!' she said in her firmest voice. 'Don't start that screaming again—you'll upset the kids still up there, not to mention the poor girl on the way down.'

The pouting mouth snapped shut and she swung around to glare fiercely at Leonie, who smiled and patted her hand.

'Good girl,' she said, defusing the anger. 'Now, do you think you could move over here so there's room for the rest of the people to land?'

'My boyfriend's still up there,' the girl said, moving obediently but turning to look back up at the swaying cradles on the big wheel.

'If he's anything like my son he's probably enjoying it,' Leonie told her. 'Thinking it's a great adventure.'

'Probably!' the girl admitted, smiling for the first time since she'd arrived back on solid ground. A soldier handed

Leonie a blanket and she wrapped it around the girl's shoulders—warmth for shock, she remembered.

The crowd was thinning, bored now that the drama was being safely defused. Alex and Leonie waited, checking each person lowered to the ground and seeing them safely into the care of friends or relatives. The growing silence indicated that the other rides had been stopped or were stopping and, although the dust was growing less invasive every minute, Leonie was relieved.

'Common sense prevailing or orders from the Army?' she wondered aloud, looking around at the still machines.

'There's very little common sense out here, you told me.' Alex's arm had reclaimed her waist and a deft manoeuvre had brought her body into close contact with his so that the words were little more than a breath of air, meant for her ears only.

'Very little!' she agreed soberly, as her tiredness dissolved in the effervescent delight of desire.

CHAPTER SIX

WITH the drama safely over, Leonie and Alex returned to their tent to find that most of their patients had left. One mother remained, holding her still-pale child in her arms while her husband went for their car.

Leonie packed some sachets of electrolyte crystals and some bottled water for the family to take with them.

'Try to get him to drink as much of it as you can,' she reminded the mother, 'then change gradually over to other fluids—fruit juices, or even fizzy drinks—but keep off milk for a while.'

The woman thanked her, and left the tent as her husband pulled up outside.

'Most people are packing up and leaving,' the soldier on duty told them. 'The locals want to get home to their properties to begin their own clean-up operations, although dust storms aren't as bad as floods or bush-fires.'

Alex seemed startled by the man's laconic acceptance of nature's vicissitudes, but Leonie was more concerned with their own evacuation than she was with the recurrent cycle of problems in the outback. The ambulance men were still asleep, but once they had headed back to Hopewell she and Alex would be alone.

The shrill ring of the cellular phone broke into her thoughts and she snatched it up from the bench, hoping that they were once again connected to the outside world.

'Had a bit of a blow out there?' Jack's voice asked.

'A bit of fun!' she agreed, so pleased to hear him that she felt a dampness in her eyes.

'You OK?'

'Tired but otherwise OK,' she assured him. 'An ambulance from Hopewell is standing by in case of an emergency but now the wind's dropped everyone's leaving so I guess they'll follow the exodus. There's no major problem, apart from the fact that Alex and I are stranded out here.'

Alex had turned as the phone rang and she saw the shadow of a smile in his eyes. Did she sound desperate?

'Eddie's on his way to get you,' Jack promised. 'He's had to go north around the cloud and will approach from the west but it may not be until first light tomorrow, depending on how high the dust cloud extends and how quickly it clears from Talgoola.'

'We'll look forward to seeing him,' Leonie replied.

But she didn't smile when Jack laughed and said, 'I bet you will!'

She wanted to get away from this place, to get away from the dirt and grit that continued to mat her hair and rub against her skin, but the balance between herself and Alex had been subtly shifting all weekend and the time when decisions must be made was drawing inexorably closer.

She closed the phone and slipped it back into the plastic bag to protect it from the dust.

'Eddie will be here late this afternoon or in the morning,' she said, in reply to Alex's raised eyebrows.

They lifted higher. Which would you prefer? they asked as clearly as if he'd spoken.

She shrugged, then half smiled herself.

'I'm so tired it doesn't matter,' she admitted. The woman and child had departed while she was on the phone, and she waved towards one of the empty beds. 'Maybe after a few hours sleep. . .'

She avoided his eyes because it was only half an answer.

'This is not the place for us!' he said quietly, moving towards her and taking her into a tender embrace so that her head rested against his neck and his vitality flowed into her body.

'Stop torturing yourself with doubts and arguments.' The deep cadence of his voice lulled her, but the teasing words that followed fanned her dancing demons. 'Don't you know that what will be will be?'

But what will be? the question mocked inside her head as she dragged her overwrought body out of Alex's arms and headed for the nearest bed. She closed her eyes on the present and shut the future from her mind, letting herself succumb to the nothingness of sleep.

She woke again to voices! She kept her eyes closed while she listened to one which was very familiar, and one which was less so but far more exciting. They were debating whether to wake her, and she solved the problem by stretching her kinked bones and saying, 'I'm awake. Eddie? Have you come to take us home?'

'Are you ready to go?' he asked, grinning at her as she shook her hair out of her eyes and blinked up at him. 'You're on holiday, remember. You could stay on.'

'In beautiful, downtown Talgoola? At the moment I feel that if I never see this place again it will be too soon. I'm more than ready to go home.'

Alex chuckled, and as Eddie began to carry their

equipment outside he whispered, 'Coward! Don't you know there's no escape?'

No escape from how he made her feel, that was certain. The mere sound of his voice teased at her nerves. She looked at him, studying his face—imprinting the smiling lips into her mind.

'I think I've got beyond escape,' she told him honestly, 'but I've no idea where we go from here—how—where. . .'

His eyes darkened with desire, but questions still flickered in their depths.

'You are certain?' he asked, in the rasping tone that played havoc with her spine.

She nodded, her mouth too dry to speak. She felt like fragile china, crazed with age, about to shatter into a million pieces if this tense expectation within her body wasn't eased. Snatch the moment, Susan had advised.

This was snatching!

'I will find a place,' he promised, his voice so full of sincerity that it sounded like a solemn pledge of more than sensory pleasures.

Their journey back to the landing strip had an air of unreality about it. The tent city had vanished, only piles of debris and fluttering bits of plastic or newspaper giving any indication that it had once existed.

'It's like a moonscape,' Alex murmured, and Leonie had to agree that it had the same feeling of desolation.

The RFDS plane stood proudly alone on the tarmac and, to Leonie, entering it was like coming home. She sank down into a seat, buckled herself in and rested her head back, glad that the disrupted weekend was finally over.

Alex hesitated beside her.

'Go up front and sit with Eddie,' she told him.

His sheepish grin told her that she'd correctly read his indecision.

'I love flying!' he admitted. 'Love all the knobs and buttons and controls. I had my licence once but don't have the time to keep my hours up these days.'

She waved him away and drifted back into a half-sleep, only stirring when she felt a change in the beat of the engine.

'Are you strapped in, Leonie?' Eddie called.

'Yes, are we home already?' she shouted back, peering out of the window but seeing no sign of the bright lights of town.

'Not home just yet,' he told her. 'We've been diverted north to Grant's Gully. Tourist hurt in a fall in one of their caverns.'

Grant's Gully? She'd heard the pilots discuss landing there in daylight, under ideal conditions. It was a short strip, with tricky updraughts caused by the ranges that ran parallel to the runway.

Eddie was their most experienced pilot—it was natural that he would be called upon to try a night landing there.

'The injured girl is still in the cavern,' Alex said, coming to sit in front of her and fastening his seat belt automatically. 'They suspect spinal injury and do not want to lift her out until they can immobilise her.'

She looked at his tired, anxious face, seeing his age in the deep lines that tracked down his cheeks.

'I'm sorry, Alex,' she said softly, reaching out to touch his shoulder. 'We seem to have thrust you from one disaster to another this weekend.'

But the lines vanished as his smile appeared and his eyes sparkled.

'You think that worries me?' he said. 'No, Leonie! I am having fun! Never have I had such fine adventures. I am thinking of asking Jack if I can work here when I take time off from the business—do locums here when doctors take their holidays.'

'You enjoyed Talgoola? Enjoyed the dust and not having enough sleep and the wailing children?'

'Didn't you?' he asked with such patent surprise that she laughed.

'I suppose I did,' she admitted reluctantly, but she knew that she'd enjoyed it because he'd been there with her, his solid, reassuring presence making the tasks seem simple and his body language taunting her with promises of what was yet to come.

The plane dropped lower, shuddered as the flaps went down, then lurched sideways before settling, as lightly as a dragonfly on a lily leaf, onto the dirt strip.

Judy Grant was waiting by the solid four-wheel drive with the National Park logo on it. Leonie freed the big Thomas pack from its moorings and Alex stood aside while Eddie hefted it onto his shoulder.

'The spinal scoop stretcher's there,' he said to Alex, pointing to where the stretcher fitted in the compact layout of the plane. 'Bring that along.'

Judy greeted Leonie with a hug.

'I'm so glad it's you,' she whispered. 'I know you won't panic.'

'Won't panic? Why would anyone panic?'

Judy stepped back and looked at her, a frown of concern between her eyebrows.

'No one's told you? I spoke to Jack. . .'

Her gaze shifted from Leonie to Alex to Eddie and then back to Leonie.

'The girl's still trapped. She's in an old lava tube. We lowered one of her friends down—a really plucky kid who volunteered—with blankets and drinks, but the hole's too small for any of us to fit through. Ben tried chipping away at it but it's ironstone—impossible—and he also realised that any pieces he dislodged were falling down onto the girl. He is waiting there, talking to them. . .'

Leonie looked at Judy, a strapping five feet ten in her socks. And Ben Grant, she knew, topped his wife by six inches. Eddie was a fair-sized man, and Alex was both tall and solid.

Jack had diverted Eddie here, knowing that Leonie would fit down the hole. She shivered in the darkness, then remembered Caroline's school visit to Grant's Gully and thought of the injured girl and her frightened class-mate. She knew she would do whatever was asked of her.

Alex helped her into the vehicle and held her hand. Her awareness of him tugged at her senses. Was he projecting strength into her? Could he do this or was she imagining it?

'We walk from here,' Judy said.

They clambered out of the vehicle and Leonie looked up at the blackness of the towering cliffs, seeing the stars like a scatter of bright stones in the velvety softness of the night sky.

She followed Judy up a narrow, unseen track through the silent bush. They climbed until her calf muscles ached with fatigue, but eventually they saw a light and came to where the scrub diminished and flat slabs of rock pressed forward to overhang the cliff.

Ben Grant was there, and the girl's schoolteacher—a plump, excitable woman in her fifties who was twisting her hands and moving about restlessly.

'You'll go down? You'll bring them both back up?' she asked.

'I'll do my best,' Leonie promised, and went forward to where Ben was explaining the situation to Eddie and Alex.

'I'll let you down first,' he told Leonie, 'then the stretcher. Alice, the girl who went down to sit with her friend, might be able to help you. She is still sounding confident, and has a good light. The ceiling's quite high where they are—'

'Which explains the patient's injuries,' Alex put in. 'If it had been a small drop she might have escaped unscathed.'

'That's right,' Ben agreed. 'No one has been in this particular tube, mainly because we didn't know it had an entrance here, but I saw the outer edge of it when I flew a mustering helicopter along the gorge one day.'

He held out a sling as he spoke and Leonie stepped into it. She had been a volunteer at enough safety equipment demonstrations to know how to fit the harness around her thighs. It would take her weight as she was lowered, and all she had to do was hold onto the rope to steady herself.

'Ready when you are,' Eddie said, as Ben wound the rope around his body to anchor it.

Alex touched her hand, then bent over the bag Eddie had carried.

'I will lower oxygen before the stretcher,' he said, taking command as if it was his rightful place. 'Any swelling in the spinal cord could impair oxygen delivery to the brain so put a mask on her immediately, then an extrication collar. You can measure the right size?'

Leonie thought for a moment.

'It should fit between the point of the chin and the chest here.' She touched her chest. 'Then rest on her collar bones and support her lower jaw.'

'Take off jewellery if she's wearing any,' Alex reminded her, and she felt herself gaining confidence from his presence, 'and get her friend to apply manual traction while you fit it. Wherever the injury is, that's important, Leonie.'

He was quietly coaching her so she could envisage each step of the operation.

'Ask her about pelvic pain. If you're in any doubt, strap her to the stretcher across her thighs and chest—not across the pelvis.' He squeezed her hand again. 'I'll talk you through it,' he promised.

She sat on the edge of the hole, dropped her legs through the narrow aperture and then wriggled her body lower and lower.

'We've got your weight,' Ben said, and she let go, feeling herself being lowered downwards in the darkness.

'You've got company, Alice,' she called, and heard the girl's sigh of relief.

'I can see you.' The scared young voice wavered, and Leonie knew that she was glad to be relieved of sole responsibility. 'When you drop a bit lower, I'll catch your legs and guide you down.'

The girl's torch gleamed briefly, then Leonie felt small hands against her calves.

'Ashley's here,' the girl whispered, shining the torch on the still form of her friend.

'Ashley and Alice?' Leonie said lightly as she extricated herself from the harness and untied the oxygen bottle and a bag with three cervical collars from the rope above her. She crossed to kneel beside their patient.

'That's how we became friends,' Alice told her, 'joking about our names.'

Then a shadow like this falls on their young lives, Leonie thought as she fitted the oxygen mask and turned on a rich mixture.

'The men will be lowering the stretcher,' she told Alice. 'Do you think you could guide it down so it doesn't crash on Ashley's legs?'

The girl was unconscious, but as Leonie pinched the skin on the back of her hand she sensed a withdrawal. Didn't that mean no damage to her spinal cord?

She glanced down at the girl's feet, but decided that she wouldn't remove her sneakers to test those reflexes.

'The stretcher's down,' Alice whispered.

'Good girl,' Leonie encouraged, setting the light down by Ashley's head. 'Now, first we put a collar around her neck to keep her head immobile.'

She studied the slight figure and chose the large child's collar from her selection.

'Now, I want you to kneel here by Ashley's head and take hold of her with these fingers under her jaw and your thumbs near her temples.'

She demonstrated the hold to Alice, then moved aside and helped the girl position her hands.

'You hold her head steady, pulling at it if you can, while I slip this collar under there and fasten it around her neck.'

'I can hold her head still, but I can't seem to pull very hard,' Alice said.

Leonie slid the tab of the collar under Ashley's neck.

'You're doing fine; hold still a moment longer while I do it up.'

She secured the collar, then reached out and touched Alice's fingers. They were ice-cold and shaking, and Leonie realised that her helper could be going into shock.

She lifted the blanket that was tucked over Ashley and wrapped it around Alice.

'Don't fall apart yet,' she said softly, giving the girl a hug and rubbing some warmth into her. 'I might need some help when they begin to lift the stretcher. I don't suppose you've got a chocolate bar in your pocket?'

Alice blinked at her, like a pale owl in the dim light. Then she patted her shorts and produced a squashed package.

'Eat it up—it will give you energy,' Leonie told her.

She left Alice and retrieved the stretcher. It would come apart so that she could slide it under Ashley from each side, then fasten it again, top and bottom, to keep it secure. She worked quickly, pushing the fine metal slats beneath the girl and matching the ends so that they fitted together.

'How are you going?' Alex's voice asked.

'Nearly done,' she told him. 'Once we have her secured, Alice and I will turn her around so the stretcher will lift from the head end.'

'Make sure the strap around her forehead is secure,' he reminded her—at the precise moment she pulled it into place.

With all the straps fastened, she slotted the small oxygen tank into place, then motioned to Alice to take the foot end.

'If you could take the weight,' she called up into the darkness above them.

The stretcher moved, and they steadied it, guiding it until it hung suspended beneath the hole.

'When you're ready for us to pull her up clip the supporting ropes nearest her head to the top frame of the stretcher,' Ben instructed. 'The foot of the stretcher will drop automatically.'

Leonie studied the stretcher and its supporting ropes. She saw the clips and realised what Ben meant.

'Could you hold it steady, Alice?' she said, and pulled the ropes sideways until she could clip the locks into place. The stretcher now hung at an angle, the foot end resting on the ground.

'We're ready,' she said, and the slow ascent began. She guided the metal frame upward, minimising movement so that the girl wasn't knocked against the edge of the hole.

'You next,' she said to Alice, indicating the sling which was being lowered again.

She helped the girl strap in, and guided her upward. Alice disappeared and in a short time the rope snaked down again.

'Alice could be shocked,' she called up as she struggled back into the sling. 'Perhaps Judy could take care of her.'

'Alex is with her now,' Ben reassured her, and she picked up the discarded blanket and torch.

'Ready?' Ben called.

'Ready,' she echoed. She thrust the torch in her shorts pocket and clipped one corner of the blanket onto the end of the rope. It would drag its way up behind her.

She reached the top and blinked in the light. The moon

had risen, bathing the bush with an unearthly glow—bright after the gloom of the cave.

'Are you OK?' Judy asked, picking up the blanket and wrapping it around Leonie's shoulders.

'Well enough to start the trek back down to the car,' she told Judy. Beyond the clearing she could see the outlines of Eddie and Alex, separated by a stretcher length, making their slow way back down the track.

'Miss Wilson's looking after Alice,' Judy assured her, 'and Ben's gone on ahead to turn the car around and work out how best to fit the stretcher into it.'

'They might have to carry it all the way down the gorge,' Leonie said, remembering the jolting ride they'd had from the airstrip.

'Alex has already suggested that,' Judy told her. 'If that's the case we'll take turns.'

It was a sobering thought but, after her feet had slipped and she'd skidded a metre forward, Leonie decided that she'd better concentrate on getting safely back down the mountain. No one would want to carry her back to the plane if she broke a leg or sprained an ankle.

Alex mightn't mind! she thought dreamily, as concentration proved elusive. Images of being lifted in his arms made her feel extraordinarily warm and comfortable, keeping her company until they came within sight of the big bush vehicle.

Internal lights showed that the stretcher had been placed in the back, with Eddie and Ben kneeling on either side of it to support it on their thighs.

'How are your knees?' Alex asked, coming to meet her as she came down the last steep pitch of the track. He gestured towards the stretcher. 'It's Eddie's idea. With you and I on either side at this end, we will act as human springs to cushion the jolting.'

She looked at him, amazed that he still sounded so full of strength and optimism.

'Will it work?' she asked.

He touched her lightly on the shoulder.

'It will help, and don't you worry about her. I am confident she will be all right,' he told her, and she wondered if he had sensed she needed to hear something positive. 'She had passed out from shock and pain when you saw her, but when we got her up she tried to struggle against the bonds. When I spoke to her she responded, squeezing my hand.'

'Oh, Alex!' She lifted her face towards him as relief flooded through her body. He touched her cheek, and she saw the bead of moisture on his finger before he brought it to his lips to taste her tear.

'Come and be a cushion,' he said softly, and led her to the back of the car, helping her into place before clambering in himself.

The drive back was slower, and fatigue cramped Leonie's muscles so that when the stretcher was finally lifted off her knees by willing helpers back at the camp she couldn't move.

Again it was Alex who helped, massaging her legs to bring the blood back into them. It was a wonderful feeling, strong and warm—yet somehow sexy—

'Ready to go!' Eddie called, and she straightened up, ashamed of her thoughts, and hurried towards the plane.

Alice had opted to return to town with them so Leonie settled her into a seat and checked that she had her seat belt fastened.

'Do you want to examine her before we take off?' Eddie asked Alex.

'No, let's get her to hospital.'

Leonie turned to show him how to fit the plane's supply of oxygen to the mask, and her fingers flashed against his arm, the soft silky hairs brushing fire onto her skin. She fought back the tremulous excitement with thoughts of work. She had stood in for nurses on evacuation flights from time to time—surely she could remember the routine!

Hospital! Ashley will need a file, Leonie thought tiredly.

She pulled out one of the big sheets and began to fill in details, asking Alice for the personal information she needed.

'Miss Wilson said she'd ring Ashley's mum and dad to let them know what's happened, and my parents, too, so Dad can meet me at the airport.'

'I'll do a full examination once we're airborne,' Alex murmured to her, taking the seat behind her and leaning forward so that she could hear him over the revving of the engines.

The noise intensified, Eddie released the brakes and they sped down the strip, lifting into the air in time for the jagged face of the deep gully to drop away beneath them.

When Eddie called the all-clear Alex rose, dictating his findings to Leonie who noted them on the chart.

'Her reflexes are still good,' he said in a puzzled voice as he returned to his seat. 'Yet Ben told me that she said she couldn't move when she first fell and they called to her.'

'She might have been winded,' Leonie said. 'And she'd have been terrified. The moon hadn't risen when I first went down there, and it was pitch dark.'

'But it was daylight when she fell—they'd climbed up to watch the sunset from the rock slab.'

'The tunnel curves around,' Leonie explained, 'so darkness wouldn't have made much difference.'

'It might if it's a hysterical neurosis,' he said quietly. 'The fall was far enough to hurt her?'

'Certainly,' Leonie told him. 'It's a wonder she didn't break her legs.'

'She may have jarred her knees and ankles, which causes severe pain, or, as you say, landed on her coccyx and winded herself. In the darkness pain and fear could easily combine to cause a panic situation. The word hysteria describes a condition, not the mad loss of control lay people associate with the word.'

'So, she didn't have to be screaming hysterically for you to think of this?' Leonie teased, smiling at the sober concern in his voice.

He smiled back and her heart went into its uneven-beating syndrome.

'Hysterical neurosis also has a state of hysterical lethargy,' he continued, his eyes daring her to laugh as he finished his explanation. 'I can't find any sign of a bump, no contusion on her head to explain concussion, so it's possible—particularly if it was dark and frightening—that her mind said "rest a while" and her body obeyed. She could wake up in hospital in the morning with only minor aches and pains from the jarring of her fall.'

Leonie seized his hand, unable to hide her relief.

'It's not certain,' he reminded her, 'but definitely possible.'

His fingers turned to grasp hers, compelling her to look at him.

'I can't keep saying thank you,' she murmured.

'And I can't keep telling you it's not necessary,' he said, then he leant forward and cut off her objections with a kiss.

It was a gentle salute at first, then warming to an urgent need that parted her lips so that tongue could parry tongue.

Her body strained against the back of the seat, wanting to be in touch with his, but only lips and fingers met, passing on messages of delight through their special sensitivity.

'We'll go away?' he muttered as they pulled apart to breathe and rest their thundering hearts.

'Whenever you like,' she whispered back, certain now that this was what she wanted. Worse than wanted—needed! she admitted silently.

'Tuesday, then?' he asked, hands clutching hers so tightly that her fingers ached. It told her of his want and need, and made her shiver to realise that it could match her own.

'I have to go back out to the university tomorrow to see the facilities and speak to the people about the work they are doing on the antibodies,' he added. 'You will come?'

She was touched that he would wish to include her in his everyday life, and excited by the other challenge he was taking on.

'I'd love to,' she said.

Night lights brightened the sky above Rainbow Bay and reflected like jewels in the waters of the bay. Darkness shrouded the runways but the air that rushed in when the door was opened was clean and sweeter than Leonie remembered. Ambulance men transferred Ashley to the waiting vehicle under the watchful eye of her parents. Alex wrote a note on the file Leonie had prepared and handed the driver their copies.

It was the usual bustle of arrival and Leonie, having handed Alice over to her dad, went efficiently about the business of straightening up the plane.

Alex's pilot met them with a briefcase full of faxes and messages relayed to his hotel in his absence. There was time only for him to press her hand, and a whispered, 'I'll phone you in the morning. Sleep well, my dear,' before he was whisked away.

CHAPTER SEVEN

LEONIE helped Eddie unload the plane, then sat down to repack all the cases, replacing drugs and equipment from their store cabinets and writing out the requisitions as she worked.

The temptation to creep home to bed was strong but an emergency could call the planes out, and she couldn't risk the staff taking a case with something missing. It took another hour to complete the final list and she locked the cabinets thankfully.

Alex had said he'd ring in the morning. Not too early! she hoped as she hurried out to her car, unlocked the door and slid into the stuffy interior. The key turned, the starter motor whirred obligingly—and nothing happened. She tried again, checked the dashboard and saw the headlight switch turned to the park position. She'd driven to the airport while it had still been dark and hadn't switched her headlights off. They turned to park when the engine was switched off, but even at that low voltage they had drained her battery.

Cursing her folly, she headed back into the hangar. Eddie had finished cleaning out the plane and had disappeared, although the plane was still on the tarmac and his car was in the parking lot.

He could be anywhere, she realised. He often wandered over to the control tower, or had a Coke with other pilots at the flying club bar. She dialled the automobile association and explained her problem, resigning herself to wait for them to come and start the engine.

It was another hour before she reached home—after midnight—and a note in Mitchell's wild scrawl was on the kitchen bench.

'Caroline at Gran's for the night, MOST exciting news for you, will tell you in the morning,' it read.

'Most' exciting news? She shook her head, too tired to think, and added her own note.

'Not before eight-thirty,' she wrote. 'I need to sleep. See you then.'

Eighty-thirty would give him time to impart his news and still reach school in time. She turned to her bedroom, had a quick shower and then slid thankfully into bed.

Her body relaxed immediately, but her mind nagged at Mitchell's 'news'. Her maternal antennae had pricked and she found the concern disturbing her sleep.

'Cup of tea! Come on, wake up! We need to talk!'

She struggled out of a deep well of restless repose and stared at her son.

Mitchell's flushed cheeks and bright eyes made her wonder why she was so certain he wouldn't touch drugs, but she ignored the signs of excitement to ask if Alex had phoned.

'Yes, ages ago,' Mitchell answered, dismissing the call with a careless wave of his hand. 'Said something about the research labs at Uni and he'd pick you up at midday.'

He was openly dismissive of this arrangement, writing it off as of no concern of his and hurrying into his real news.

'But something much more important has happened,

Mum. I didn't want to spoil the surprise by telling you in my note. Guess what?'

She hid her disappointment at missing Alex's call and looked properly at her son. Excited wasn't the word for it. He glowed! He shone! The energy within seemed to ripple from his skin!

What could it be? She tried to think, but in the end she had to shrug and shake her head, smiling at his suppressed delight but completely bewildered about what might have caused it.

'Wait two minutes while I wash my face, then tell me,' she said, touching his hand in the hope that she might help him down from this ebullient high. She dragged her aching body out of bed and to the bathroom, too bemused to begin to guess what was happening.

'*Dad* phoned!' he announced as she returned, seizing her in his arms and dancing her frozen body around the room. 'Isn't that great! Dad *phoned*!'

Denial hammered in her head, but she found the strength to pull away from him.

'Dad? Your father phoned?'

She stared at Mitchell in horror, then sank down onto the bed before her knees gave way completely.

Her mind tried to absorb it all at once. Not only disbelief that Craig had tracked them down, but stunned amazement at Mitchell's reaction.

She'd start there.

'Mitchell Cooper,' she said severely, mustering her scattered wits, 'you have spent the last twelve years of your life telling people that your father is dead because you refused to accept that he'd left us, and now you're telling me he rang! And you're *excited* about it!'

Defiance tilted his shoulders back, and anger rippled in his eyes.

'He didn't leave us! He came back but we'd shifted!' His voice rose and she remembered how young he was—and how little he knew of her tortured and tortuous relationship with Craig! 'I remember telling you we shouldn't have gone away. I told you Dad wouldn't be able to find us when he came back, and that's exactly what happened! He's been looking for us ever since.'

She remembered the tearful little boy who'd raged at her, but she couldn't let that memory weaken her.

'For twelve years, Mitchell? We're still in Australia. Don't you think he might have found us earlier if he'd been serious about it?'

'We lived in Melbourne, Mum!' he argued. 'Rainbow Bay is as far away from there as you can get without crossing water!'

He was parroting Craig, and she could almost hear his calm, reasoning voice—making intricate excuses, telling such plausible lies! The thought that he had found them made her shiver. What did he want? And why now?

She shut her eyes and tried to think.

It had to be money. Craig had only ever come home when he'd wanted money. She'd thought she'd left him enough more than twelve years ago when she'd made her escape—left him the home her father had paid for, and all their furniture, plus one hundred thousand dollars from the sale of her mother's home. Buying peace with money and threats! Twelve years of peace.

'Where is he?' She looked around almost fearfully, as if he might appear from behind the door. Or was it his influence over Mitchell that she could feel?

'He's driving north,' Mitchell told her sulkily. 'He'll be here late Tuesday. I asked him why he didn't fly and he said he couldn't afford it!'

His grey eyes glared their reproach at her but, beneath the shock and horror she was feeling, she knew she had to fight back. She straightened in her chair and frowned at the son she loved so dearly.

'Don't try that guilt trip on me, Mitchell. Your father walked out of my life too often for me to pay to welcome him back.'

She paused, drawing a deep breath to calm the tremor in her voice.

'He is your father, and I know how much you loved him. Because of that, I've never loaded any of my past, or my memories of him, onto you or Caroline. You're welcome to see him, and I'll be pleased for you if it works out and the two of you get on together, but leave me out of it.'

'But he can stay here, can't he, Mum? I told Dad he could stay here! He said he was sure you wouldn't mind—that you were too. . .' he hesitated as if trying to remember the words '. . .too civilised to mind.'

He watched her warily as he spoke, trying, as all children did, to gauge a parent's mood—ready to draw back at warning signs that he'd push too far or too hard. And while she battled to marshal her thoughts into understandable sentences he tried a smile—always a good tactic, she remembered from her own teenage years!

'Anyway, Mum, you're on holiday—you could go away if you don't want to be here with him.'

A logical thrust! She stared at the boy-man in front of her and stifled a bitter smile. She'd been worrying about

Mitchell's reaction to her going away with Alex for a few days, and here he was—unwittingly shoving her into Alex's arms.

But her stomach churned at the thought of Craig in her home. It had been her refuge, her sanctuary—and it was no longer safe! Mitchell was watching her warily. It was his home as well, she reminded herself.

Then she thought of her daughter, a laughing two-year-old when she'd swept her children north. Caroline had no recollection of her father, although she probably believed the litany of 'Mr Wonderful' stories Mitchell had passed on to her over the years.

'Does Caroline know?' she asked.

Mitchell made a noise she knew was a yes, but looked uncomfortable. She waited, knowing that he was honest enough to tell her what was troubling him.

'Gran was here when Dad rang! She got upset and said I shouldn't have spoken to him, shouldn't have asked him to stay.'

It's getting worse! Leonie realised. She should phone her mother immediately. Upset wouldn't begin to describe the effect the news would have had on her!

'Was Caroline concerned about it?' Leonie persisted, digging at the embarrassment that lurked in Mitchell's eyes.

'Well, she said she didn't care if he came or not because she couldn't remember him, but I shouldn't upset you. Then she took Gran home to settle her down and said she'd stay with her!'

Great! Take a little interlude all for yourself, and the heavens fall down on your head!

She stared at the cold tea, then looked up at her tall son.

'Hop off to school,' she said in her everyday 'mother' voice. 'We'll talk this afternoon.'

He was walking out of the door when her mother phoned, her voice stiff with anger. Leonie listened, letting her finish her tirade before she tried a little cooling logic.

'Mitchell's entitled to see him, Mum,' she said. 'Although he's denied his existence for so long, I've always thought he'd want to find him—one day. Craig was a good father to him.'

'When he was there!' her mother muttered. 'When he deigned to come home and needed someone adoring to hang off his every word. You'd grown immune to his charm so he used it on Mitchell instead.'

'It took me four years to grow immune to it, Mum,' Leonie pointed out.

'For all of us!' her mother snorted. 'We all fell for the good-looking devil!'

Regret and sorrow intermingled in the older woman's voice, but Leonie knew there was strength there as well—and a determination that matched her own when it came to protecting her family.

'Well, what are you going to do?' her mother said into the silence. 'You know Mitchell's asked him to stay?'

'Not indefinitely, I hope! My instinct tells me to run away—go somewhere until he gets bored with playing Dad and disappears again.'

Silence greeted that remark. Her mother knew as well as she did that Craig Cooper wasn't driving thousands of miles up from Melbourne to reacquaint himself with his children. He wanted something and, although she didn't know what, she knew him well enough to know that he'd use the children as a lever. But a lever for what? She had nothing to give him!

'I'm sorry, Mum, what was that? My mind's stopped working.'

'Go away,' her mother repeated. 'As you say, Mitchell is old enough to make his own decisions. Caroline wants to stay here anyway, and I'm quite willing to take her over to visit him if she wants to see him.'

'I can't ask you to do that,' Leonie groaned, although escape was infinitely tempting.

'I'd like to do it, love,' her mother said softly. 'I'd like to prove I can stand up to him now, and if I'm at all worried about the situation I'll get Susan to come with me. Caroline has already told Stewart her father's coming, and he's offered to stick with her when she sees him. He's a sensible young man.'

Leonie groaned. That was another problem! She'd been fighting a losing battle against Caroline's interest in Stewart Stone, telling her that she was too young at fifteen to commit herself to one boyfriend. But the Stones were such close friends as well as work colleagues, and the children had grown up together. When Stewart's twin, Lachlan, had been in hospital both her children had haunted the corridors, but while Mitchell had visited Lachlan Caroline had comforted Stewart and their relationship had begun to change.

'I'll have to think about it!' she said. 'I'll phone you later.'

'You didn't sleep well?' Alex's fingers brushed across her cheek-bones, lingering on the bruised shadows beneath her eyes. His voice was so full of sympathy that she wanted to rest her head on his shoulder and howl like a hurt child.

'Strange bed!' she joked, turning away from his delicate caress and staring out of the window. She'd read enough magazine articles to know that a man didn't want to be burdened by his mistress's family problems. Not that she was his mistress yet!

He didn't probe but drove his hire car efficiently across to the university, parked it neatly in a spot marked VISITORS and came swiftly around to open her door.

She pretended not to notice the hand he reached out to her, and climbed out swiftly—unaided. Although she suspected that Alex's little courtesies were an inbred part of the man, as natural to him as breathing, today they made her wary and uncomfortable. They were uncomfortably reminiscent of Craig, who'd used them to convince people how charming he was—part of his clean-cut, handsome façade that had hidden a mass of dark contradictions.

'You know many of the people at Coorawalla have the encephalitis antibodies in their blood?'

She glanced at him, grateful that he was perceptive enough to see she needed something to divert her mind.

'I'd followed things that far,' she agreed. 'But you need a live virus to work from, and for that you need to find a carrier—isn't that right?'

He smiled at her and she sensed a little of the excitement that had driven him to scientific discovery rather than hands-on medicine.

'If possible!' he replied. 'But here at your university they are working backwards—starting with the antibody that makes some of the islanders immune to the virus and seeing if they can replicate it.'

'And your team?' She was drawn willingly into the

discussion. Far better to think about encephalitis than Craig—although he was probably as potentially lethal, she thought grimly.

'They will work on the island, continuing the search for the live virus.'

The words rang with a determination that made her smile. She felt the tension easing in her neck and hurried along beside him, eager to begin the tour—to become part of this search that had brought him back to Australia.

'And will they find it?'

He must have heard the teasing note in her voice for he hesitated and looked into her eyes.

'That's better,' he said softly, trailing the back of his hand slowly down her cheek.

She stared at him, knowing that she had been ill at ease since they'd met this morning but not realising until now how in tune he was with her moods.

'I believe they will!' he added, his eyes gleaming conspiratorially at her.

He took her hand and led her into a small laboratory, calling greetings to the three people who were working at the benches.

'Medical research has changed since Edward Jenner scratched a child's arm and infected him with cowpox,' he explained, 'but the work we do remains the same. You take a hypothesis, then set out to prove it right or wrong.'

Edward Jenner—smallpox! Leonie tried to think back to student days when she'd studied the development of vaccines.

'But is there a correlation?' she asked. 'I thought smallpox was wiped out because it only occurred in humans—there were no animal carriers or reservoirs.'

He beamed approval at her.

'Exactly! We could also eliminate measles and are having some success with polio for the same reason,' he said. 'This is partly because the immunity is long term but also because these diseases don't affect animals so, with a worldwide campaign of inoculation, they could cease to exist.'

He led her to a refrigerated cabinet at one side of the laboratory, opened a drawer and carefully pulled out a slide.

'I'll show you the antibodies,' he said, as excited as a child showing off a new toy!

With precise simplicity, he pointed out the differences between this and other cells in the blood and went on to explain how antibodies work, locking on to viral cells and rendering them impotent. She remembered enough pathophysiology to know there were complicated processes behind this simplistic explanation, and that some cells were used specifically to alter the programming in other cells, but for the moment it was enough to know that the antibodies protected those who carried them from the disabling and often fatal disease.

'And are you doing all this work to prevent a disease that affects a handful of people every twenty years or so?'

He chuckled quietly.

'Worried about my profits?' he asked.

She looked at him, blank-faced with shock! Had her questions sounded mercenary? Was Craig infecting her with his way of thinking before he even arrived at the Bay?

He took her arm and led her towards a small office, divided off from the laboratory by glass partitions. Once inside, he waved her towards a chair, and propped himself against the desk, looking down at her as he explained.

'My company spends millions each year on research, and quite often it leads nowhere. But one day we might find an inoculation against cancer, and the profits from that would pay for more research into other things. We work more on prevention than on a cure, and do not have to sell our products for a fortune because we mass-produce and sell so many, making a little on each one.'

'But MVE exists in such a small area of the world—is it worthwhile your wasting time on it?'

She hoped that she sounded scientifically interested—because she certainly didn't feel it. Alex's presence had pushed her fear of Craig to the back of her mind, and her body was again responding to the powerful personality of this man who lounged so easily in front of her.

'MVE is related to a number of other viral encephalitis strains. Earlier in this century a particularly virulent strain swept across China, then spread to North America and Europe. It was labelled encephalitis lethargica because of the feeling of lethargy among the sufferers. And, like anything that causes damage to the brain, the ongoing costs of rehabilitation, health care and support are enormous.'

'So, one inoculation might work on other forms of the disease?'

He smiled and shook his head.

'Not so far!' he said, then he waved his hand towards the white-coated assistants, 'but we're working on it!'

He settled himself more firmly on the edge of the desk and reached out to take her hand.

'Now! Enough of that talk! What I wish to discuss is us.'

'Us?' she echoed faintly, forgetting that only yesterday she'd agreed to go away with him.

His fingernail scraped against her palm, and images of Craig faded further into the background.

But should she take her mother's advice? Go away and leave her children to face this unknown father? Mitchell might be excited at the prospect, but Caroline?

Alex was talking and she tried to concentrate on his words. Something about Turtle Island.

Turtle Island? She'd seen pictures of the cabanas set amongst tree-studded lawns. And the pool that wound like a fresh-water creek through the property so each suite had its private swimming area. White coral sand and translucent water—the stuff of dreams.

Face realities! her mind reminded her.

'It's too expensive,' she told him. 'I can't afford it. But we could go to one of the other islands, or up north to one of the beach resorts.'

'You can't afford it?'

He emphasised the 'you' enough to make her feel uncomfortable.

'Of course I can't, Alex,' she said crossly. 'I'm a sole parent, supporting two teenagers who have all the expensive tastes of their ages. You've got Carlos—you must realise that the only shoes teenagers can possibly pull on their feet have a big name brand slashed across them and cost three hundred dollars. And all their other clothes are governed by the same trends. On top of that, Mitchell goes to university next year. He wants to study medicine in Brisbane—probably to get away from his mother. It's going to cost a fortune!'

'But I would pay,' he said solemnly, and, suspecting he might be laughing at her, she tried to read the expression in his eyes.

'I don't want you to pay!' she snapped. 'I'm the one who suggested we have an affair. If anything, I should be paying for you!'

His eyes gleamed and she knew that he was laughing, although his beautiful lips remained gravely still.

'It's better if we each pay our own!' She blundered on, trying to ignore the wild tumult in her body caused by nothing more than the silent messages from his eyes and the finger tickling at the palm of her hand.

It's impossible—especially now, she told herself, and felt the fires die down, killed by the trepidation she felt for her children—and her own relationship with them.

'Anyway, I don't know if I can get away after all,' she said bluntly.

She looked up at him, wondering if her eyes reflected the misery she was feeling.

'I knew something had happened to upset you. Was it Mitchell or Caroline? Did you speak to them about me? Are they so against our seeing something of each other?'

Sympathy and understanding oozed from his voice, making her feel warm and protected, but she couldn't hide behind the children this time.

'It's not them,' she said bluntly. 'Well, it is, but not to do with you and me. It's something else—they might need me.'

She couldn't explain about Craig, couldn't face admitting how foolish she had been—how naïve, how gullible, how humiliatingly trusting!

'I also need you, Leonie,' he said quietly. 'And I think you might need a little of yourself—a time to be a person, not a mother.'

How I wish! she thought, but the temptation of his words provoked more anger.

'You can't stop being a mother simply because you want to,' she told him forcefully. 'It's not a responsibility you can dump when it becomes bothersome!'

His smile curled its way into her heart, and when he reached out gentle fingers and smoothed them over her hair she felt like crying.

'It's what I love about you, this fierce determination to do the right thing!' he murmured. 'This single-mindedness when it comes to what you perceive to be your duty—whether to your job, or to your family. It is admirable, Leonie, and—to me—very, very attractive!'

What I love about you!

It's a turn of phrase, nothing more!

But he'd used the word!

Not outright!

Voices argued in her head, but her demons had whirled back to life.

Love didn't matter, she reminded herself. All she wanted was a brief affair—an interlude—remember?

Then she heard an echo of Mitchell's voice...'I told Dad he could stay here!'

And her mother...'I'd like to prove I can stand up to him.'

Poor Mum, she'd adored her son-on-law and had refused to accept the dark side of Craig—blaming Leonie's indifference for his infidelities—until the uncles had provided irrefutable proof that he'd been manipulating company funds to pay for the string of beautiful women he'd chased so tirelessly.

She looked into Alex's dark eyes and reminded herself

that it was a strong physical attraction she felt for him—something exciting and different and special—but not love. Love caused pain, and she'd been there—done that!

'I'll sort things out at home—I'll make the time to get away,' she promised. 'But not Turtle Island—somewhere I can afford. I'll do the booking, if you like. When do you go to Coorawalla?'

His eyes had lost the golden lights and were darkly watchful.

'Friday,' he answered easily enough, though Leonie felt a shifting in his mood. 'I'd have to be back in town on Thursday to check on the arrangements and meet the research team. If we leave tomorrow morning we'd have two nights.' He paused, frowning at her, then added, 'And *I* will make the arrangements!'

Sound pleased, or excited, or lover-like again, she wanted to cry—but she was being businesslike and matter-of-fact, so why wouldn't he be?

A call from the laboratory took Alex away, and Leonie picked up a book on antibodies and immunology, finding refuge from her thoughts in the continuing eradication of diseases. Because the encephalitis was carried by mosquitoes, the area covered by the Rainbow Bay Base was particularly vulnerable to MVE and the recent outbreak had worried all the staff.

'So, you've learned something?' Alex asked when he returned some time later.

'I have, in fact,' she told him, fascinated in spite of her other concerns. 'Did you know that once about seventy per cent of the population is immune to a particular disease then the disease finds it hard to survive? What percentage of the people of Coorawalla had antibodies?'

'Not quite enough,' he told her, chuckling at her enthusiasm. 'Although I did know that!'

He took the book out of her hands and closed it, then presented the front cover for her inspection.

Puzzled, she read the title, then embarrassment heated her skin.

'So you wrote it! Of course you knew!'

'As you know about your service,' he reminded her. 'I'm pleased you're interested because my work is an important part of my life.'

'But I'm not part of your life, Alex,' she argued. 'Not in any ongoing sense!'

He brushed his fingertips across her shoulder and she knew that he saw the instant tremor in her skin.

'So you keep telling me,' he murmured.

CHAPTER EIGHT

ALEX dropped Leonie home at four.

'Dinner tonight?' he suggested.

'No,' she said reluctantly. 'I'd better remind my children what I look like.'

'Then I'll phone you later and let you know what time we're leaving in the morning.'

The words triggered all her internal excitement and, as his lips brushed hers in a quick farewell, she was tempted to forget her children and go with him now—back to his hotel—anywhere! As long as they could be together and she could ease the agony her newly awakened senses were causing.

He let her go, seemingly as reluctant to part as she was, but she knew that she had to replenish the food supplies and tidy the house before she could go away again.

And speak to her children!

Was that why the temptation to stay with Alex had been so strong? she wondered as she unlocked the front door. Was he offering an emotional as well as a physical escape from the reality of her life?

She pushed inside, trying to see her house through a stranger's eyes. Lime-washed cane furniture with bright cushions gave the big living-room an air of cool, but casual, comfort. Craig would hate it, she knew. He preferred rich elegance, fancy furniture that told visitors of the occupants' wealth—not their personality.

Yet it was a home that invited people in, that provided security for her children and a welcoming haven for their friends.

Haven?

She could hear the argument as soon as she was properly inside, although the door to Mitchell's room was shut. She knocked and opened it, and Caroline flung herself forward, burying her tear-stained face against her mother's breast.

'Caro's carrying on about Dad,' Mitchell said, his defensive shell fully erected and challenge gleaming in his grey eyes.

'She doesn't have to see him if she doesn't want to,' Leonie said quietly, rubbing at her daughter's shoulder in a soothing motion. 'It's her decision, Mitchell.'

'But he'll be disappointed if she's not here.'

Leonie quelled the 'Tough!' that rose to her lips, saying instead, 'He'll live with it,' in her driest voice.

Mitchell glared suspiciously at her, but Caroline had recovered sufficiently to speak.

'I haven't said I won't see him,' her plaintive voice explained. 'I said I'd think about it, and if I decided I would then Gran would come with me.'

Leonie saw Mitchell's lips thin, and his face took on his mulish look.

'Dad said Gran never liked him much.' He glared at his mother. 'He said all your family were against him!'

Oh, boy! This is all I need—an argument with my son over my family's behaviour to his poor, hard-done-by father! She couldn't blame Mitchell. Craig had always been able to put over a sob-story with hints rather than accusations!

'Gran loved your father,' she said quietly. 'We all did—at first. My father and his brothers took Craig into their business; they helped him all they could.'

She hesitated. Where did you draw the line in explanations like this? How should she portray Craig without destroying Mitchell's idealistic view of him when she knew that such a destruction would lead to Mitchell hating her and not his father.

'He had a weakness,' she said carefully. 'And it led him into trouble. I won't say more than that, Mitchell, because you must judge him for yourself. But you love your grandmother and you've always been fond of your great-uncles in Melbourne. Remember that when you listen to your father's stories.'

'Tell us what happened,' Caroline begged, but Leonie shook her head. These two were the last people with whom she would want to share those years of hope, and shame, and—eventually—utter despair.

'It would be unfair to let what happened between your father and me influence you, Caroline,' she said. She stroked the golden hair Caroline had inherited from her father, then added, 'He had his faults—and so did I—but I think he genuinely loved you two.'

There you are, Craig, she told the ghost that hovered in the room. I can't do more for you than that. She even half believed it—mainly because she couldn't think of any other reason he could be heading north.

'Now, come on, both of you. Who's going to help with the shopping, and who's offering to vacuum instead?'

The tension diffused, she took Mitchell off to select the food he thought his father might fancy. Maybe two days of pizza and potato wedges would send him scurrying back to Melbourne!

Caroline had dinner at home, then returned quite happily to her grandmother's. Leonie washed the dishes, puzzling over this. Was Gran allowing her more private time with Stewart? She was frowning as the phone rang, but when she heard Alex's voice she told herself that it was a worry she could sort out later in the week!

'I will collect you at six o'clock. We must get an early start.'

His enthusiasm bubbled in the words, exciting her out of her doubts.

'An early start to where?' she asked.

'A secret destination,' he told her huskily. 'Private, secluded—'

'Not Turtle Island?' she demanded suspiciously.

'I was going to add—and cheap!' he said, pretending to be hurt by her suspicion.

'I need to leave a contact number with the kids,' she told him, and he gave her the number of his mobile phone.

'But tell them the number is for emergencies only. You need a proper holiday—from *all* your cares! I have told my pilot, who acts as my secretary on these trips, the same thing—"Interrupt me at your own risk," I said to him.'

'No phone calls! What bliss!' she sighed, then smiled. 'And no dust?'

'Definitely no dust!'

'It sounds idyllic,' she told him. 'Six o'clock, then!'

He repeated the time in a voice that rustled over her nerves like satin across skin, stirring the tiny hairs on her arms to attention and sending blood pounding through her breasts—her thighs!

Alex had hired a catamaran, and for two days they had lost themselves in the maze of islands within the sheltering arms of the Great Barrier Reef. Clear water washed on white coral sands; tall, jungle-clad mountains rose up from purple depths of sea; sea birds swooped above them, and dolphins rose and dived across the prow of their lazily moving vessel. It was a heavenly setting, but the beauty and pleasure of her surroundings could not surpass the passion, the delight, the sensuous magic of their love-making.

'I don't want this to end,' Leonie murmured as she lay in his arms on Thursday, knowing that they would have to head back to the Bay very shortly.

'It doesn't have to,' he told her, raising himself on one elbow so that he could look down into her face. 'Stay with me for ever.'

She blinked at him because 'for evers' had never been mentioned.

'It's impossible,' she reminded him. 'We live half a world apart. Mitchell and Caroline—their lives are here. Mitchell's plans for university—Caroline must finish school!'

She raised herself to kiss his slightly parted lips, tasting the exciting masculinity that could drive her to a frenzy of love then reduce her to quivering weakness in his arms

'It's been wonderful! More special than I could ever have imagined, but it never had a future, Alex—we both knew that.'

'Did we?' he said, pinning her back on the bed with

one hand on her shoulder and trailing the fingers of the other around her breast. 'I know, my lovely woman, that you went on and on about affairs, and secrecy, and different worlds, but I don't recall agreeing with you.'

He bent his head and nipped lightly at her nipple so she had to fight her physical responses to him as well as the seduction of his words.

'The world is small in these days of jet travel so half a world is nothing.'

He transferred his attention to her other breast, then used his fingers to slide the moisture he'd left around her peaked nipple.

'Mitchell is leaving home to go to university next year, anyway,' he continued, his tone as bland as if he were discussing stock prices or the weather, while his fingers teased and squeezed so that she had to bite back the moaning anguish of her desire. 'So he come can come to you during his holidays, wherever you might be. And we do have schools in Switzerland. Caroline would be happy there. She liked my Carlos when they met before. He would be a brother to her—introduce her to his friends.'

Temptation fluttered like a light-blinded moth in the hidden recesses of her body, but it was too simplistic.

'They might not want to move. I don't speak Italian, which I know you speak in your part of Switzerland. I wouldn't fit in, Alex, and the kids would probably hate it, and I'd be overwhelmed with guilt.'

She squirmed beneath his questing fingers and made a half-hearted attempt to push his hands away.

'I have a good life here,' she told him. 'I feel safe and content.'

His hands flew outward in an exclamation of horror.

'Content!' he yelped. 'That's not enough! You must feel alive and excited, and look forward with great eagerness to each new day.'

He bent forward and kissed her on her lips.

'I know your "content" for I had it myself for many years. With Carlos's mother, I worked hard, building up my business, and came home at night to my lovely wife. I was content.'

Another kiss, more insistent than the previous one.

'But now I have success, and need to spend less time at work. When I moved my factory from Italy to Switzerland I made much money because the old property—on the lake so we had water supplies—had become very valuable. So now I have the leisure to do things that please me and the money to indulge my pleasures.'

'Like this?' she teased, for, in spite of his wealth, she couldn't picture him as an international playboy.

'Like this with you,' he said, his eyes dark with other messages. 'But, for myself, it is being able to indulge in research at Coorawalla; to play Flying Doctor for a while if Jack will allow it. I like doing things, Leonie, being involved, and I believe you share that liking. How much greater is a pleasure shared?'

Husky voice against her skin, seductive words filtering into her mind.

'We hardly know each other!' she argued, falling back weakly on convention.

His laughter trailed across her nerves, while his fingers teased her with their intimacy.

'Could we "know" each other much better than we have these last few days?'

Anticipation meshed with caution, and he must have

sensed it in her slight withdrawal from his touch for his fingers splayed across her stomach, stilling the tremors.

'I'm here for a month,' he reminded her. 'I won't rush you into a decision. Just promise me. . .' a pause as lips met '. . .you'll think about it, and tell me all your thoughts.'

Again his lips brushed hers.

'I won't have you worrying over something that could be worked out between us.' His eyes burned down into hers. 'Even "home" need be no barrier, my love. Should you decide that it's physically impossible for you to move I'll move myself—reorganise my affairs so much of my work can be done from here.'

Another kiss, another soft caress of fingertips. 'But, be warned, I will steal you away whenever I can. I want to show you all the places I love—see your eyes light up at the beauty of Sacre Coeur, watch you dive beneath the sea in the Bahamas and marvel at the majesty of the Iguacu Falls.'

Leonie closed her eyes. It sounded like commitment—like love, almost—and she was tempted to give in to it—to place her future in Alex's hands and let someone else make all the hard decisions.

'I have to think!' she told him, remembering that love had never been mentioned except in the heat of their passion when both of them had used the word with feverish urgency. And she didn't want love!

'I'll let you think,' he promised, then he stroked her hair back from her face and kissed her eyelids, her nose and chin.

'Do you think you could do some of the thinking at Coorawalla?'

She smiled, and reached her arms around his shoulders to hug him.

'You'll have your employees there,' she reminded him. 'And Carlos!'

He sat up, drawing her up with him so that he could hold her and look into her eyes.

'It would be my privilege to show you off to them,' he said.

It must be love, she thought, as a piercing sweetness flooded through her.

'My future wife!'

She looked at him, stunned by the assumption.

'Wife?' she gasped, and he teased her with his smile.

'Would you have us live in sin? What kind of example would that be for our impressionable children? Of course you will be my wife,' he promised, sealing his words with a deep, throbbing kiss. 'It is only the matter of when that we must solve. If necessary, I will wait, Leonie, until your fledglings have left their nest.'

He kissed her again, smothering her arguments with the intoxication of his lips.

'But I won't wait quietly. I will batter at your defences—remind you daily of these few short days, of what pleasures we are missing, what bliss we could be enjoying.'

Her mind whirled into chaos, his words like a web that enmeshed her senses. To be with Alex all the time! The lure of travel failed to move her, but the subtle pleasures of sharing mealtimes, discussing his work or hers, their children's futures—these enticements were hard to ignore.

Love hurts! her head reminded her. She twisted out of his arms, and hurried into the bathroom.

They were under way by the time she was showered and dressed. She joined him in the cockpit, and he put his arm around her as they motored back into the bay, their bodies touching. Replete—for the moment.

'Do you want me to come in?'

They were outside her house and she knew that he was offering to stand by her while she spoke to the children.

'No, Alex, I will tell them in my own way.'

But tell them what?

He had driven away before she remembered Craig—before she realised that she had not thought of him since Alex had swept her into his arms on Tuesday morning.

Maybe he was gone. Then she saw a strange car with Victorian number plates parked a little further up the street, and her body grew cold. He hadn't gone!

Mitchell must have heard the car drive away for he opened the door as she walked up the path. His face looked strained and tired, and she felt a wave of guilt that she'd left him to face his father alone.

'Dad's sick,' he announced. 'I was going to phone, but you said you'd be back today.'

Leonie stood on her front doorstep and tried to assimilate both the spoken and unspoken messages.

The accusation in Mitchell's eyes told her that he was holding her responsible for his father falling ill—a child's view that it was her fault for not being here and preventing it! But the tremor in his voice told her that he was confused and frightened. For his father?

She reached out and hugged him. It didn't matter what he feared—her instinct was to reassure him.

'We'll look after him,' she promised, then she handed him her bag and walked inside.

Craig *was* sick. She looked at the man who lay in her bed, his eyes closed against the light and his breathing ragged and harsh. He was older, of course, and some of the glow had gone from his golden good looks. She backed out of the doorway.

'Ring Dr Halligan's surgery, Mitchell. Ask them if someone's available for a house call.'

'I rang them earlier,' he said. 'Dr Halligan's off duty today, but they'll send someone after surgery.'

Leonie glanced at her watch. It was barely lunchtime! Four or five hours to wait, depending on how overbooked the GP's afternoon session was.

She went back into her bedroom, and walked cautiously across to the bed. A dozing crocodile wouldn't have instilled more fear in her as her shaking hand reached out to touch Craig's forehead, and her fingers felt for a pulse in his wrist.

He was burning hot, and his pulse tumultuous. She found a damp face-washer, and her heart contracted as she realised that Mitchell must have been using it to cool his sick father.

She took it into the bathroom to wet it again, then laid it on Craig's forehead. It was never going to be enough. She hurried out of the room again to find Mitchell, hovering outside the door.

'Did he tell you how he felt? Where it hurt? Was he physically sick?'

'He was sick all through the night—I heard him.'

'Did he take anything, then?'

Mitchell began to look sick himself.

'I didn't get up,' he admitted, guilt flushing his cheeks to scarlet. 'I thought it was the drink. He'd had a few beers, then quite a bit of wine and some of that brandy you got for Christmas—'

'It's OK,' she said gently. 'There wouldn't have been anything you could do for him at that stage. And this morning?'

'He said he had a terrible headache and I gave him two painkillers out of our cupboard, the ones you give Caro when she has a migraine. They didn't seem to help and he said his neck was stiff so I rang the doctor.'

Severe headache and sick stomach could be a hangover, but the stiff neck and temperature were more worrying. And was he sleeping off a bender, or was the deep sleep something more sinister?

'I think he should be in hospital where they can do tests.'

'He said you'd send him to hospital to get rid of him!'

The accusation shot across the room, but before she could defend herself Mitchell was speaking again.

'I wanted to ring you this morning but he wouldn't let me. I thought maybe Gran could help but he said she'd get rid of him too—that you didn't want him here—that you'd probably—'

The sentence ended abruptly, but the anguish in her son's eyes made her ask, 'Probably what, Mitchell?'

He hung his head, hesitating, so that she had to ask again—in her most implacable, not-to-be-denied voice.

'Probably poisoned the brandy!' he muttered, then hastened to add, 'But he was only joking.'

He lifted his head and she saw the unspoken plea—the 'wasn't he?' that he hadn't said.

Had he not taken action in case she had poisoned the

brandy? Had he been afraid for her?

'Of course he was,' she said briskly. 'What time did he take the painkillers?'

'Eight o'clock! That's when I decided to stay home from school.'

Any palliative effect would have worn off. She thought for a moment. Much as she would have liked to bundle him into hospital, Mitchell would see her action as a confirmation of his father's words. She would have to nurse Craig through the afternoon and hope that the GP would insist on the man being moved to specialist care.

'Well, I'll take care of him now,' she assured Mitchell. 'Why don't you have a sleep?'

He smiled for the first time since she'd returned home.

'Maybe I will,' he said.

She watched him head into his bedroom. The poor kid would have been drained by all the emotion of meeting his father again—then to have him fall ill!

She found two more of the strong painkillers, then headed back into the bedroom. Craig looked as if he was sleeping but she was relieved when he roused to her voice.

'Beautiful as ever!' he murmured, looking up at her with eyes dulled by the fever.

'As I recall it, you preferred brunettes. Blondes were too insipid for your taste.'

He smiled, but the rearrangement of his facial muscles didn't bring any warmth to his eyes and she reminded herself that a sick animal was often the most dangerous.

'The doctor can't get here until later,' she said briskly. 'You'd better tell me how you feel, where it hurts—that kind of thing.'

'I thought nurses were supposed to do hands-on work!' he complained.

'Not this nurse! Now, you're obviously running a temperature, and Mitchell says your head aches. What else?'

'I ache all over, you unfeeling woman!' he complained. 'And my head doesn't ache, it pounds incessantly and there's a huge invisible giant squeezing my temples.'

She was half-inclined to smile, but he'd always used humour to defuse her anger and she sidestepped his trap.

'Here, take these. Have you had a cold, or any flu symptoms?'

He struggled into a sitting position and tried to catch her hand as she passed him the tablets. Was it all an act to prolong his stay in her house?

'I'll tip the water over you if you try that trick again,' she told him, passing him the glass so that he could wash down the medication.

He blinked at her, and she wondered if she'd been so spineless years ago that such a small act of defiance surprised him.

Probably, she decided as she picked up the washer and headed back to the bathroom. Why else would she have put up with his infidelities for so long—his flaunting of the other women in his life?

'Here, put this on your forehead,' she suggested.

It wouldn't do much to reduce his fever, but it might ease his headache. She should sponge him down, but she wasn't about to get that intimately close to him!

He fell asleep again, and she slipped out to buy some juice and fruit, returning home in time to greet Dr Halligan's offsider.

'It's my ex-husband,' she explained. 'He came up to

visit the children while I was away on leave.'

She was skating recklessly around the truth.

'Mitchell says he was vomiting in the night. He's been complaining of a headache and a stiff neck, and he seems hot and feverish.'

She opened the door to her bedroom, and let the doctor go in alone.

The phone saved her from following. It was Caroline, asking if she could stay another night at Gran's.

'I did call in and meet him, Mum,' she explained earnestly, 'but I think it will take me a bit longer to decide if I want to know him any better. It's OK for Mitchell because he sees him as a mate. They can have drinks together and stuff like that!'

Oh, can they now? Leonie wondered, but she understood what Caroline was saying.

'You stay on with Gran, pet,' she said easily. 'Craig's not well, and I wouldn't want you catching whatever he has.'

They chatted for a few minutes, then said goodbye, and it wasn't until she had hung up the phone that she realised that neither of her children had asked her about her holiday! Was Alex right? Had she let her life be ruled by their needs and concerns for too long?

She tried to avoid the thought, but it followed her into the kitchen where she leant against the bench and longed for Alex—for the feel of his strong arms around her waist, for the solidity of his broad shoulders to rest her head against.

'I think it's a bad dose of the flu,' the doctor informed her, poking his head into the kitchen. 'I've given him a penicillin injection, and here's a script for capsules. Start him on them at ten tonight, then two every six hours. There's another script for painkillers—the instructions are there, but no more than two every four hours of those, either.'

Oh, what fun! she thought, but she took the scripts and thanked the young GP.

'Call the after-hours service if he doesn't improve,' he added, as she walked him to the door.

Back inside, she checked the patient, who was sleeping, then cooked a chicken casserole for dinner. It was Mitchell's favourite dish, and she smiled as she watched him devour his helping, then clean up the leftovers. The drama of the past few days hadn't ruined his appetite.

'I've got to run into the after-hours chemist in town to get this script,' she told him. 'Craig should sleep, but if he wakes there's juice in the refrigerator and you could ask if he'd like a cup of tea or something light to eat, like toast.'

'Right, Sister!' Mitchell saluted cheekily, and the knot of anxiety in Leonie's chest began to ease.

She was gone for over an hour, the queue in the chemist shop testifying to the prevalence of the flu virus doing the rounds.

'Dad stayed asleep,' Mitchell told her when she got back. 'I looked in a few times.'

He leant forward and kissed her cheek.

'I'm off to bed,' he announced, and she looked at him with a wry affection.

'Typical male!' she muttered. 'Hand over all responsibility to the nearest woman and take yourself off to bed!'

'Well, you can go to bed now,' he reminded her.

'In Caroline's room, where your father should be! And

for how long? I have to give him tablets at ten, then more at four in the morning.'

Mitchell reached out a hand and ruffled her hair.

'Set the alarm,' he suggested with a cheeky grin. He headed into his bedroom, shut the door, then reopened it to say, 'Oh, and Alex rang while you were out. I said you could be ages and asked to take a message, but he didn't leave one.'

The door began to close again, then he hesitated.

'What's he ringing you all the time for?' he asked, not quite suspicious—yet! 'Aren't you supposed to be on holidays?'

Several replies flashed through her mind.

Because he wants to marry me! Rejected—too much traumatic shock.

Because he's interested in me! Rejected—hoots of laughter likely to greet it!

'He's a friend,' she said mildly. 'We enjoy each other's company. We like to talk.'

'Well, you'll be too busy to talk to him with Dad sick.' Her son dismissed Alex with his deadly teenage logic. 'See you in the morning.'

She'd give Craig his ten o'clock tablets and then ring Alex, she decided. And after he'd shored up her flagging courage she would sit down and work out exactly what she was going to tell her children about this relationship.

It was an unpromising thought to take into the sick-room, and the last she had for some hours.

Craig was thrashing around on the bed, bathed in perspiration and muttering incoherently, and she forgot her reticence and fetched a bowl of warm water to sponge his heated body.

He quietened enough for her to give him the tablets, then he drifted off into a restless sleep. She sat and watched him for a while, arguing the case with herself.

The doctor would have hospitalised him if he'd thought it necessary. Was Craig right? Was she thinking of hospital as a way of getting him out of her house? What would Mitchell think if he woke and found his father gone?

She fetched fresh water and sponged Craig down again, surprised that she could carry out the task without thinking of him as a person at all.

Seeing him quiescent, she slipped away, had a shower and pulled on a nightdress. If he was still asleep she'd go to bed, setting the alarm for four when his next tablets were due. At least she'd get a few hours sleep.

But he was too restless for her to leave him, so she pulled one of the cane armchairs into the room and settled herself uncomfortably into it, dozing from time to time but waking when he cried out—to bathe him again and feed him sips of water.

At four the fever seemed to break, and he settled into a deeper sleep. Exhausted by the demands of the night, Leonie pulled a light blanket around her shoulders and crept into Caroline's bed, falling asleep as soon as her head touched the pillow.

'Mum, he's much worse and Dr Halligan's rooms say they can't get anyone here until lunchtime.'

Leonie struggled back to consciousness, and peered at her watch. It was eight-thirty! Some nurse she'd turned out to be.

She hurried into the bedroom. Craig's face was flushed, his eyes half-closed, and little moaning sounds were issuing from his lips.

She reached for the phone and dialled the Base.

'This is Leonie, Sally. Are any of the doctors in at the moment?'

'Jack's here. I'll switch you through to him,' Sally said briskly.

'Could you come up to my place, Jack?'

'I'll be right there!'

Her body shook with relief.

'Is he coming? You didn't tell him why!' Mitchell's voice cracked on the words and she longed to hold him and comfort him, but a wall of suspicion still barricaded her out.

'The thing about good friends is that you don't have to explain,' she said quietly, and saw his nod of acknowledgement.

They heard the car pull up outside and the sound of footsteps—voices. Voices?

Mitchell was welcoming Jack and saying hello to someone else, then Alex's arm was around her shoulder, steadying her.

'Is it Caroline?' he asked, his voice rough with concern.

Speechless, she shook her head then stepped out of the tender curve of his body.

She seized Jack's hand and dragged him into her bedroom, only too aware that she was still in her nightdress, her hair tousled from sleep, and she hadn't told Alex about her husband reappearing in her life!

'A doctor saw him last night and said flu,' she told Jack. 'He put him on antibiotics but he's been feverish all night. I thought yesterday he should go to hospital but. . .'

She couldn't explain the 'but'!

Jack had crossed to the bed and was already examining

Craig. Leonie was aware of Alex's presence in the doorway. She could feel him there as definitely as if he were touching her. Could even hear his thoughts as he looked from the man in the rumpled bed to her, and back to the bed again.

And, in case he was in any doubt at all, Mitchell chose that moment to explain, 'It's Dad!'

CHAPTER NINE

'PHONE an ambulance!'

Jack's order distracted her from the problem of Alex, and she brushed past him, heading for the phone in the living room. Her fingers were shaking so badly that Alex, who must have followed her, took the receiver and said, 'Is it 999 or 000 in Australia?'

'It's triple zero,' she told him, her voice shaking as much as her fingers. 'And the address is—'

'I know the address, Leonie,' he said coolly.

She heard him pass on the relevant information, then he replaced the receiver and turned towards her.

'It's your ex-husband? He's been visiting the children while you were away?'

It would be so easy to nod, but memories of the lies that had destroyed her marriage held her motionless.

'He's not actually an "ex" husband,' she told him, and saw the shock in his eyes and read anger in the slow stiffening of his body.

'No wonder you couldn't give me an answer yesterday. No wonder you needed time! Time to dispose of one husband before you took on another!'

She stepped towards him, and touched his arm.

'It's not like that!' Her fingers tightened, as if she could impress her words through his skin. 'I haven't seen Craig since I came to Rainbow Bay—twelve years ago.'

'Yet you remained married to him?'

Splinters of the ice from his voice pierced her heart.

'I had a reason. I will tell you. . . Should have talked about it. . .'

She looked into his face with pleading eyes.

'We've had so little time together—how could I spoil it with the unhappiness of the past?'

She wondered if his eyes had softened, or whether hope had helped her imagination conjure up that impression?

The arrival of the ambulance cut off any further talk and she waited silently while Craig was carried out.

'You'll go with him, Mum?' Mitchell said, his voice thick with the tears he was battling to control.

Leonie looked from her overwrought son to the man she knew she loved and nodded, her heart so heavy that she wondered how it could keep beating.

'I'll get dressed and drive straight over there,' she promised. 'Why don't you get off to school? It will take your mind off things, and I'll phone you there if there's any news.'

He swooped on her and hugged her tightly.

'I'll ride up to the hospital after school,' he promised, and then, with a final hug, disappeared into his bedroom.

Jack, who had followed the stretcher, reappeared in the doorway.

'Alex and I were having an early meeting when you rang. I suppose we'd better get back to it.'

She reached out and took his hand.

'Thanks for coming, Jack,' she said. 'Mitchell had rung our GP but all their staff were busy until lunchtime.'

'Home visiting is what we're good at,' he reminded her, then he leant forward and kissed her cheek, before heading for his car.

Leonie looked at Alex, who was following Jack out to the car.

'Alex. . .'

Her hand reached out, then dropped back to her side. He turned his head briefly towards her, and she felt his glance rake over her from the top of her dishevelled head to the tips of her bare toes.

'You'd better hurry. They'll want your husband's details when he gets to the hospital.'

And he followed Jack swiftly out towards the car.

Somehow she survived the day. Lists of tests were ordered, beginning with blood but progressing rapidly to spinal taps. Leonie, obedient to Mitchell's pleas, sat outside Craig's hospital room while staff withdrew cerebro spinal fluid and talked of meningitis.

'We're pumping high-dosage antibiotics into him, but if we can identify a specific organism we can direct our therapy more specifically,' an earnest, white-coated young man explained. 'Of course, the CSF doesn't always show a clear diagnosis of meningitis immediately so we retest if we're uncertain.'

She listened to the words, but couldn't assimilate them, except the frightening information that they were keeping Craig in isolation.

Some bacterial forms of meningitis were extremely contagious. She remembered that much from her studies. And Mitchell had been nursing his father.

Severe attacks of meningitis could cause brain damage.

Her worry grew until it enveloped her.

'My son was with him,' she told the young doctor next time he appeared.

'And yourself?' he asked.

She nodded briefly, and waved that concern away. 'Should Mitchell be tested?'

'Not yet, but I'll get some antibiotics for both of you to take as a precautionary measure.'

She sank back down into the chair and tried not to think of the disappointment she'd seen in Alex's eyes. All the 'if onlys' hammered in her head, and no amount of argument could make her believe that those few days together were enough to count as the 'interlude' she'd wanted.

And Alex was off to Coorawalla today!

The thought pushed her out of the chair and she prowled down the hospital corridor, looking for a public phone. She would explain what had happened—he deserved that much. Whether he believed it or not was a different matter.

The phone was in a corner by the lifts, and she dug in her purse for change, fed the machine and dialled his mobile number.

'Alex Solano's phone, but he's not taking calls unless someone's dying!'

The voice was a lighter, younger version of Alex's deep tones.

'Is that you, Carlos? This is Leonie Cooper.'

'Ah!'

A knowing sound, then silence. Leonie waited for words that didn't come.

'Just "ah", Carlos?'

'Well. . .'

She knew she shouldn't pressure him. They'd become friends, she and the young man, when she'd visited him in hospital after his diving accident, talking to him on the two-way while he lay in the hyperbaric chamber.

'He's in a mood, Leonie!' Carlos finally admitted.

'I knew he would be,' she said unhappily. 'Would you. . .? Could you ask him if he'd speak to me?'

There was another pause.

'I'll see! I'm at the hotel but we've got a suite and I'm in my room. He mightn't be in his.'

Carlos was making excuses in case he refused, she realised, her heart pounding with anxiety.

'I'm sorry, Leonie.' The apology sounded heartfelt and sincere. 'He's not there!'

Anger replaced the anxiety.

I should have lied to him this morning!

Carlos was speaking again but the blood drumming in her ears blotted out his voice.

'Goodbye, Carlos!' she said abruptly, and hung up the phone.

She walked back to Craig's room, and looked through the window to where a masked nurse was bathing him. The woman finished her task, checked the IV line and bag, then stripped off her gown and mask and slipped out of the room.

'He seems less restless,' she said. 'Why don't you go down to the canteen and get something to eat?'

It seemed like years since she'd eaten so she took the woman's advice and made her way downstairs.

Familiar faces greeted her, but she could only respond with a distracted nod. She couldn't face the social chit-chat of the hospital. The 'Who's sick? One of the children?' that politeness would insist that she answer.

Down in the canteen she chose a salad sandwich, then carried it and a foaming mug of tea outside into the sunshine. A patch of grass beneath a low-limbed cassia provided shade and privacy, and she sank down and unwrapped her picnic.

She must have eaten before she'd gone to sleep because ants were crawling on the discarded plastic wrap and her teacup had only a few drops of liquid in the base of it.

Gathering up her rubbish, she hurried inside. It was after three and Mitchell would be here before long. She could imagine his disgust if he found that she'd neglected her promise to stay with his father.

It was strange how she was automatically thinking of Craig as Mitchell's father! Perhaps if she could continue to consider him that way she could accept him as an ongoing part of Mitchell's life!

She left the lift and walked slowly back towards the isolation rooms. It certainly seemed as if Mitchell wanted him in his life.

Yet trepidation shadowed that thought. She tried to tell herself that it was jealousy—that Mitchell's sole allegiance belonged to her—but she knew that wasn't true. She had brought up her children to be independent of her and to give allegiance to those they grew to know, to like, to trust—

Trust! With Craig so sick, she'd forgotten her initial suspicions. Why had he come north? Why had he sought them out?

'There are flowers for you.' The nurse she'd spoken to earlier stopped her as she walked past the ward station. 'The junior is putting them in water.'

'Can you put them in Mr Cooper's room?' Leonie said. 'Unless I can go in now?'

'Oh, they're not for Mr Cooper, they're for you,' the woman said. 'A gorgeous-looking man brought them. I told him you'd gone down to the canteen. Did you see him?'

Leonie had only begun to assimilate this information when the junior appeared with a vase of yellow roses.

Love washed through her, flooding her being with an incandescent joy.

Ignoring the proffered flowers, she raced back to the phone and dialled Alex again.

'Carlos, standing in for Alex!' the cheeky voice told her.

'Was he really not there when I rang earlier?' she demanded.

'Of course he wasn't,' Carlos told her, his injured innocence practically melting the phone wires. 'Would I lie to you?'

If you had to, yes! she thought but only asked, 'Is he there now?'

'I'm sorry, but he hasn't returned,' Carlos told her. 'Can I get him to call you back?'

'No, I'm at the hospital,' she explained. 'But would you thank him for the flowers and tell him. . .'

How much did Carlos know? Had Alex told him any more than she'd told her children?

'Tell him I'll try to phone him later.'

'We're off to Coorawalla in an hour,' he said cheerfully. 'I don't know if our cellular phones work out there.'

They don't, Leonie thought gloomily as she headed back to take up her unwilling vigil once again.

By eight o'clock that evening she had convinced Mitchell that his father was in good hands and persuaded him that they could safely leave the hospital. She carried Alex's roses out with her, but Mitchell made no mention of them.

'He said he hasn't many friends, Mum,' her son said sadly as they drove homewards.

She glanced at him and realised there was no blame in the statement. She'd have liked to have told him that friendship couldn't survive betrayal, but as she'd made a point of never denigrating Craig to his children she could hardly knock him while he was down.

'He moved about a lot when he was a child,' she said, offering the only explanation Mitchell might find acceptable.

'Yes!'

The monosyllabic reply made her wonder. The fizzing excitement Mitchell had portrayed after his father phoned was gone but whether sobered by the man's illness or damped down by knowledge, she couldn't tell.

Her mother and Caroline were waiting when they arrived home, and her bed was made up with fresh, clean sheets.

'Thanks, Mum,' she said, giving the woman who had helped her through so much a special hug.

'It's nothing, dear,' her mother said, then waited until the children had gone to their rooms before talking about the one thing on both their minds.

'He's up to something,' she announced, her stout frame tight with indignation. 'I saw him and he said he'd had an urge to see his kids, but he didn't answer when I asked why now, or how he found out where you were.'

'Well, he can't do much from a hospital bed,' Leonie assured her, although her mother's words started all her doubts jostling in her head again.

'And Alex?'

Her mother nodded at the roses. She had encouraged

Leonie to explore her attraction to Alex, pooh-poohing the idea that her daughter was too old for romance.

'He was here this morning,' Leonie admitted. 'With me in my nightdress and Craig in my bed! Great fun, that was!'

'You *have* had a day!' her mother said quietly, then she reached out and kissed her.

'Seize whatever happiness you can,' she told her. 'You've given enough of your life to those kids. They're old enough to stand on their own.'

'Like you did, Mum?' Leonie teased gently. 'I don't remember you telling me that your life was in Melbourne when I decided I had to get away and came up here. I don't remember you saying that I was old enough to stand alone—and I was older than my two.'

'There'll always be times when you need a mother,' her own dear relative replied. 'I'm not suggesting you abandon your two completely, just let yourself have a life outside of theirs. You can't deny I do that.'

Leonie chuckled. Her mother played golf two days a week, bridge another two, swam with the Masters Swimming Club and had recently taken up line-dancing at the local hall.

She watched her go, then checked the children, stopping for a quiet word with Caroline who was feeling guilty because she hadn't fallen for her father's charm as heavily as Mitchell had.

Alone at last. She unplugged the phone from the living-room and carried it into her bedroom. Alex's headquarters at Coorawalla were in the newly rebuilt hospital. She'd try to get him there.

'It's like old times,' he murmured when a messenger

had brought him to the phone. 'Conducting my courtship by phone.'

'A radio phone,' she reminded him. 'I know one island where the phone conversations were picked up on the television sets for months before the problem was sorted out.'

'So, be circumspect!' he murmured, his voice saying all the things words couldn't.

'Thank you for the flowers,' she began, knowing that words were needed. 'I'm sorry about this morning—what you thought, what you must have felt. It was so bizarre, the whole situation.'

'Jack told me he had never met the man—that he'd assumed he was dead.'

So Jack had saved the day!

'Mitchell used to tell people that,' she explained. 'He couldn't believe that he would have left voluntarily.'

They were skirting around the real issue, she knew. Because it was possible that others might hear, or because it was a delicate subject for a phone conversation?

'But why no "ex"?' Alex asked, and she realised that it was the possibility of eavesdroppers, not the delicacy, that was bothering him.

'I ran away,' she admitted, pleased that he couldn't see the flush of shame the words brought to her cheeks. 'I did everything but change my name in the hope that we could stay undiscovered. I didn't need to be free so I didn't apply for freedom. It would have meant communication—revealing where we were.'

She heard a growl of anger over the phone and the harsh question, freed of all restraint, 'Did he abuse you? Threaten you? Hurt you physically?'

'I can't discuss it, Alex,' she whispered as her heart filled with happiness that he cared. 'It's been over for a long time now.'

But was it? Until she knew why Craig had come to Rainbow Bay, would it be over?

'You'll get the necessary papers—go ahead now there's no reason to hide? Shall I get you a lawyer?'

She smiled at his eagerness.

'I'll sort it out,' she promised, then remembered that an official divorce made little difference to the decision he wanted her to make.

She asked about his accommodation, the research team, and Carlos—easy conversation to round off an uneasy day.

The diagnosis of bacterial meningitis was confirmed and, for Mitchell's peace of mind, Leonie continued to visit Craig. He was so insistent that someone remained with his ill father that she had to wonder if some of his concern was guilt. Had he not fallen prey to the charms of the man?

'He's worse!' Mitchell declared when he arrived next afternoon to see his father—still in isolation—lying limply in the bed, his neck extended so that he looked as if he was peering up towards the ceiling.

'Now they've isolated the bacteria they've changed the drugs. He'll be all right, but it could take time.'

'Will it leave after-effects? If it's a brain fever will it affect his brain later, like encephalitis?'

Mitchell had been one of the students chosen to go to Coorawalla to take blood from domestic livestock in the search for the carrier of the MVE. His interest in medicine had led him to read all he could about the disease.

'It affects the meninges, the membranes between the

skull and the brain. Encephalitis affects the brain itself. With any severe illness, there's a possibility of after-effects.'

She hoped he'd stop there but, after another long look at his father, he turned back to her.

'Like what?' His eyes were locked on hers, seeking signs of any evasion.

'I can't remember all of them, and they are only possibilities anyway. I know partial deafness could occur, there could be organ damage or arthritis.'

She was certain there were other complications and was thankful she couldn't remember them. That was more than enough worry for Mitchell to handle at the moment.

'None of this need happen,' she added, 'particularly if your father was fit and healthy before he picked up the virus.'

The days dragged on. The isolation was lifted and, against her will, she moved from her perch outside the door to a chair beside the bed, reading to Craig from magazines when he was awake and restless.

'You don't have to do this!' Alex told her angrily when he phoned at nine one evening and she was already in bed, drained by the daily stress of sitting with the man who'd caused her so much pain.

'I'm doing it for Mitchell,' she said, and heard his answer in the silence from the other end of the phone.

He thinks I do too much for the kids, she thought miserably, and wondered if he was right.

'Could you take some time off for me tomorrow evening if I fly back across to the mainland?'

'Oh, Alex! What a wonderful idea! Mum will sit with Craig if Mitchell insists. When will you come?'

'Let Mitchell sit with him!' he said gruffly. 'I'll fly back after lunch, go out to the university for a few hours and then collect you at your home at—say, five o'clock? We can drive up to The Cove, have a walk on the beach and a quiet dinner at one of the waterfront restaurants.'

The thought filled her with such happiness that she knew it was time to speak to Mitchell and Caroline about her feelings for Alex. She scrambled out of bed and went through to the kitchen to make a pot of tea.

It should be whisky to give me strength! she thought, considering whether this was best done singly or would they feel more secure if they were together.

She called them out, and sat them down in the living-room—both expectant—Mitchell nervous.

'It's not bad news about Dad, is it?'

'No,' she assured him, and looked from one to the other, praying that they would understand. 'It's about me.'

Mitchell eyed her warily, but Caroline smiled so sweetly that she wondered what Gran had been saying.

'You know I've been seeing Alex Solano since he came back to Australia.' Bored nod from Mitchell, and excited wiggle from Caroline. Try again, Leonie, she encouraged her failing heart.

'Well, we like each other. Very much, in fact!'

Caroline got up from her chair to fling her arms around her mother's neck.

'Oh, Mum, that's wonderful! Will you marry him?'

Across Caroline's shoulder Leonie watched her son. His expression, one of bored indifference when she'd made her announcement, changed to one of total disbelief at Caroline's suggestion.

'He's Italian, he lives in Switzerland. How could Mum possibly marry him?'

How indeed? she thought drearily.

'Is it only where he lives that worries you, Mitch?' she asked, using the diminutive of his name she'd used when he was tiny, her eyes on his unhappy face.

'No! You're not his type! He's a rich, successful jet-setter. If he's talked about marriage he's probably conning you. He's after a bit of a fling while he's in Australia! You're such an innocent, Mum! You'd fall for anything!'

'I'm thirty-eight,' she argued, shifting so that Caroline could squeeze into the chair beside her. 'Old enough to know my own mind!'

'That's just the point, Mum,' Mitchell declared, his voice softer now, as if he was genuinely concerned for her. 'I mean, you're not old, exactly, but don't you think a man like Alex would go for someone younger?'

And sexier? More beautiful? She heard the other—unspoken—objections quite clearly. He likes *me*, she wanted to say, but Mitchell's words had brought her own doubts back to the surface, although she knew that he was using what seemed like rational arguments to hide his own uncertainty and fear.

'Well, nothing's decided,' she said, returning Caroline's hug, 'but I'm going out with him tomorrow night and I wanted you both to know about it. We'll talk again.'

'You're going out with him while Dad's still in hospital?' Outrage glistened in his eyes.

'Yes, Mitchell,' she said firmly. 'And I'm leaving at five so if you feel someone should be with your father you'll have to go and sit with him. I notice your visits have been getting shorter and shorter lately!'

Mitchell started to speak, defiance stiffening his lean frame, but she cut him off.

'I've been visiting your father for your sake, not for his,' she pointed out. 'I don't like him, Mitchell, not at all, yet I've sat there because you were unhappy about him being on his own. I will continue to visit him for you, but I won't be made to feel guilty when I'm not there, Mitch. That is moral blackmail, and it is particularly unattractive.'

She walked back into her room, more upset than she had been since the whole ridiculous episode had begun. What had happened to her carefree, uncomplicated life? Her contentment?

The evening with Alex renewed her strength and courage. With smiling patience he listened to her objections to their marriage, then pointed out rational and logical solutions to each one. But it was his presence which revitalised her—the simple fact of being with him made her heart beat faster, her brain work more clearly and her senses more appreciative of all she saw and heard and tasted.

They walked on the beach after dinner, their shoes dangling from their fingers so they could feel the crunch of sand between their toes and the warm, tropical water lap against their ankles.

'Whitehaven Beach?'

He whispered the name of the beautiful white coral beach where they'd made love one night during their cruise. The moon had turned the water to a silver mirror, edged with the diamond sparkle of the sand. They'd built a fire and cooked lobster over the flames and then, drunk on the beauty of the night, had wrapped their bodies together in the ultimate closeness.

He drew her into the shadow of a broad-leafed coconut palm and kissed her deeply, awakening the physical memories of that night.

'I should go home,' she whispered, a kiss away from wanting more than he could give on this less private beach. Would he suggest they go back to his hotel suite? Was Carlos with him?

'Perhaps that is a good idea,' he said, brushing his lips along her jaw-line. 'It is still early and I could reacquaint myself with your children.'

Shock drew her back. It was a sensible idea but procrastination had never seemed so appealing.

'Come!' he said softly, but she knew that the decision had been made. That softness hid the formidable strength of steel. Alex Solano hadn't become successful by avoiding challenges or skirting delicate issues.

She called out as she came into the house, letting Caroline and Mitchell know that she was home.

'Shh!' Mitchell erupted from his bedroom, a finger to his lips.

'What's wrong now?' Leonie demanded in a quieter voice. 'Is Caroline sick?'

Caroline emerged from her bedroom, her usual healthy looks answering the question.

'Mitchell's put a woman in your bed!' she declared, the remnants of a bitter argument with her sibling still hanging in the air between them.

'Well, it was a man last time so I suppose I should be pleased he's shown more discretion!'

Alex's amused voice reminded her of his presence and

she turned to him, then back to the children.

'You remember Alex,' she said weakly.

With perfect aplomb he reached out to shake Mitchell's hand, then took Caroline's and raised it to his lips.

'Carlos hopes to see you both while he is here,' he added. 'He'll have a week in Rainbow Bay when he returns from Coorawalla.'

Leonie watched, part amused, part anxious, as her children responded politely to Alex's opening gambit. At least they weren't so overwrought that they'd forgotten their manners.

'Now, about this woman?' Alex asked, stepping closer to Leonie and putting his hand very lightly on the small of her back.

We are in this together, he was saying both to her and her children. It wasn't an overtly lover-like touch, but she found it comforting.

'It's Dad's wife!' Mitchell muttered, and Leonie was glad of Alex's support.

'His wife?' she echoed weakly and saw Mitchell wriggle his shoulders, indicating supreme discomfort with the situation.

'Well, you'd been gone twelve years so you'd have expected him to remarry, wouldn't you?' He defended his absent father, but she sensed a despair beneath the words and wanted to reach out and draw him close. With sudden clarity she realised why he was so upset. The child in him had hoped for a fairy-tale ending. Ignoring twelve years of no contact and all common sense, he had hoped that his parents would get back together again.

'I'm very glad he's found someone else,' she said, not adding that she'd never doubted it. In fact, he'd always had someone else. 'But what's she doing here?'

Caroline took up the explanations.

'He was supposed to phone her every night and when he didn't she panicked and hopped on a plane, then got a taxi out to our place because that was the only address she had.'

'And you put her to bed in my bed?' Leonie prompted, and the defensive look came back to Mitchell's face.

'She was exhausted after travelling all day. I told Caroline she should have given her her bed, but she refused so what could I do? I knew you wouldn't mind sharing with Caro. It's probably only for one night.'

'It's definitely only for one night!' Leonie told him. There was an edge of admiration in Mitchell's voice that told her that Craig still had an eye for attractive women. For a moment she wanted to scream with frustration. Why should all this turmoil be ruining the brief time she had with Alex, and confusing her so much that she couldn't begin to think about the future?

'Go back to your studies, or bed,' she told them. 'We'll sort this out in the morning.'

Mitchell disappeared so quickly that she knew he was glad to escape, but Caroline lingered long enough to give her mother a kiss then turned to Alex, her cheeks flaming as she muttered, 'I think it's great about you and Mum!'

CHAPTER TEN

'BUT it is wonderful news that he's remarried. Could he have divorced you without you receiving papers?' Alex's arm curled around Leonie and his voice curled into her ear.

'I don't know the legalities, but I suppose there's some provision made to enable people who can't find their spouses to divorce them.'

'But you don't sound happy,' he objected, turning her so that he could look into her eyes. 'Are you upset Craig's remarried? Do you love this man still?'

She looked up into his eyes, alight with bright flecks of anger ready to flame at one wrong word.

She smiled her reassurance, although in her gloomy state it was an effort.

'They mightn't be legally married,' she pointed out. 'I can't believe anything he did could work out well for me!'

'We can find out,' he announced. 'If he divorced you records of it will be somewhere. I have a man in Melbourne who will find that out for us tomorrow so you needn't discuss it with him—or with her. Now, why don't we get this woman out of your bed? I will arrange a room for her at the hotel.'

His arms had crept around her while he was speaking, but at this suggestion she pulled away.

'No way!' she said. 'I won't have you spending money on my problems. I can deal with this myself.'

He smiled and leaned forward to kiss her on the nose.

'The money would mean nothing to me,' he argued.

'That's the point,' she retorted. 'Like Turtle Island! The fact that the money means nothing to you doesn't make it more acceptable. I don't want you to feel you have to buy me—that your money will make a difference to my decision.'

He caught her in his arms, his breath coming out in a little growl of love, and she was able to forget all her troubles while she sheltered there.

'Will you allow my money to make our marriage easier?' he asked gruffly, when both of them were breathless from their kiss. 'Allow me to use it to fly you to the children or them to us, wherever we may be? Can you see it is money that could make a compromise between our lives possible?'

'Yes!' she breathed against his shoulder. 'You can use your money for that.'

She knew it was an answer to his other question—the proposal. They still had to sort out when, and how, but the yes was implicit in her words. Now that she had known his love, she knew she couldn't live without it.

'I'm feeling sick!' a querulous voice cried from her bedroom.

Leonie broke guiltily away and hurried towards the door.

A beautiful brunette graced her bed, wearing, Leonie realised crossly, one of her favourite negligées.

'What kind of sick?' Leonie asked.

The brunette's dark eyes shifted from her face, and her attitude changed. By shifting imperceptibly she was able to reveal large areas of sun-tanned breast, while her eyes took on a soulful, yearning look that made Leonie want to throw something at her.

Alex had obviously followed her into the room! This... this *creature* would hardly be baring her bosoms for Caroline or Mitchell.

'Pains in my stomach,' she murmured, placing a hand high enough in that region to give the overlarge mammary glands an upward push.

'The bathroom's through there if you want to be sick,' Leonie said, forcing the words through tightly clenched teeth.

'I might have what Craigy's got,' the little-girl voice whimpered, never taking her eyes off Alex.

'Or, with any luck, it might be rabies!' Leonie muttered under her breath.

'What are your symptoms?' Alex broke into the conversation, his voice so bland and 'doctorish' that Leonie felt a surge of relief.

'Just sick in my stomach,' the woman said. 'But Craigy was feeling sick in his stomach before he left Melbourne so it could be what he's got.'

No wonder he was feeling sick if you called him Craigy all the time, Leonie thought, without a shred of sympathy for this latest unwelcome guest.

'Perhaps we'd better send her straight to hospital,' she suggested to Alex, who grinned as he read her true intentions.

'I think perhaps a little bi-carb soda for now, and hospital in the morning if she shows any other symptoms.'

He drew her out of the room.

'She's an exhibitionist, I'd say,' he murmured. 'I'd

ignore her unless she becomes seriously ill, and if that happens call an ambulance.'

He drew her into his arms again.

'Would you like me to stay?' he asked.

'More than anything!' she told him. 'But I think it might complicate things even more, and I've as many complications as I can handle at the moment.'

She reached up to brush a kiss across his lips.

'Besides, don't you have a pile of paperwork waiting for you in your hotel room?'

'I have,' he admitted, 'but it would wait longer if I thought you needed me.'

'Need you? I ache for you,' she admitted, blushing as she heard such brazen words issue from her lips.

He returned her kiss.

'But now is not the time. I know that! Phone me in the morning. I go back to Coorawalla at nine, but can return at any time.'

They parted reluctantly, and Leonie watched him drive away, ignoring the demands for attention that were issuing from her bedroom.

She didn't know how, but she would make things work between them; make it possible for all of them to be happy—she and Alex, Mitchell and Caroline, and, of course, Carlos! She hadn't begun to think through his side of things!

She turned back inside, mixed some bi-carb soda in boiling water and took the drink into her house guest.

'Alex is a doctor. He suggested this,' she said, setting it down with exaggerated care on the bedside table.

'He should have examined me,' the woman said.

'He's not practising as a doctor,' Leonie informed her.

She gathered up some clean clothes and a less glamourous nightdress, then said firmly, 'You may stay here tonight because Mitchell offered you a bed, but tomorrow I will drive you up to the hospital to see Craig and you will have to make your own accommodation arrangements. The patient welfare officer at the hospital will help you.'

'But I've no money,' the woman wailed, and she sounded exactly as Craig had sounded back in the days when he'd come slinking home and she would try to send him away.

'I don't fall for that line any more!' she said crisply. 'Tell the welfare officer—she'll fix you up.'

'He said you were a cold, unfeeling bitch!' The woman spat the words out and Leonie turned away, colliding with Mitchell as she came out of her bedroom.

'How dare she say that to you!' he fumed, and Leonie felt a thrill of shock that her son, with all the contrariness of his age, had switched sides again.

'She's upset. Don't worry about it. I'm not!' she assured him. 'But she goes tomorrow, Mitchell! No more invitations to either of them!'

He hung his head for a moment, then reached out to give her a tight embrace.

'I understand, Mum,' he whispered.

The day began badly when her uninvited guest protested about getting out of bed before midday.

'I'm going up to the hospital now, and if you're not ready in five minutes you'll be walking,' Leonie told her firmly.

They left an hour later, but at least the woman—now

introduced as Deanne—understood that the move was final and took along her suitcase.

'But you'll have to show me his room,' Deanne protested when Leonie drew up at the main entrance, removed her suitcase from the boot and headed back towards the driver's seat.

'Ask at the front desk,' she suggested. 'I've run out of "nice" for the moment.'

She drove off, feeling strangely triumphant that she'd finally stood up for herself. She stopped at the Base, hoping to see Jack and explain why she'd felt it necessary to call him before sending Craig to hospital.

'Boy, am I glad to see you,' Susan greeted her. 'Can you spare a few hours for a mercy mission? I was about to phone the agency to see if I could get a nurse, but you know the equipment so much better.'

Leonie frowned at Susan, ensconced behind the desk in her office.

'What's the panic?'

'It seems one of those refugee boats has run aground on the north coast of Herd Island. Someone off it was well enough to get across to the settlement and raise the alarm, and a search party has set out. Eddie's flown the big plane out with quarantine officers and Nick and Jenny on board, and he's radioed in to ask for another plane. The poor blighters have landed in crocodile-infested swamps. There are stingers in the water, and mangroves for miles and miles—so it's hardly good walking. Michael's on an evac with Kelly and Jane—road accident victims they're taking straight to Brisbane. I've got Bill standing by at the airport, but. . .'

She shifted slightly and thrust out her leg, revealing a much-scribbled-on plaster cast.

'When did that happen?' Leonie demanded. 'Why did no one tell me? And what are you doing at work? Is it broken? What did you do?'

'Starting at the end, I fell down the back steps, broke a bone in my foot and twisted my ankle, and it happened last weekend and no one told you because we knew you'd react exactly as you are reacting and insist on coming back to hold the fort! We even swore the kids to secrecy, but the doctor wants me to keep it dry so I can't go trudging through mangrove swamps.'

She grinned at Leonie, then added, 'And your doctor is back on Coorawalla, isn't he? I won't be taking you away from time with him.'

Leonie shook her head, then nodded, totally bemused.

'I'll go to Herd,' she said. 'But could you phone my kids and let them know? If they could stay at your place I'd be grateful. I don't know how much you've heard about the goings-on at home, but every time I leave my house Mitchell puts someone in my bed!'

Susan grinned.

'I've been following the saga. I'll insist they come to me. Maybe you'll have an hour or two to fill me in when this trip is over.'

'A day or two, more likely, if you want to hear the whole story!'

Leonie left, hurrying out to her car and driving direct to the airport.

'Jack phoned through and told me what to load,' Bill said when she arrived, to find the plane waiting. 'He thought we'd have an agency nurse who wouldn't know where to find the gear.'

'That saves me a job,' she told Bill, and climbed into the plane, her thoughts already on the boat people.

'You'd think they'd stop coming, when so many of them get sent back,' Bill said as they took off over the cane fields.

'But imagine how bad conditions must be in their own country for them to risk their lives in unseaworthy old vessels, and travel through such dangerous waters with little or no knowledge of navigation.'

They flew over the deceptively placid waters of the gulf towards the large island that was Herd. Tidal swamps made most of the land unproductive, but fishing tribes had lived there for generations. By the time they touched down the boat people had been located by one of the boats, searching the inhospitable coast.

'Jack's on his way, and there's a boat waiting to take you around there,' the driver, waiting at the airfield, told her. 'You're to take the equipment bags, and he said to tell you to make sure you've got a mask and gloves unless you want to go into quarantine with them.'

'Will we be flying the people to the quarantine station at Darwin?' she asked as they drove towards the pier.

'Don't know!' he told her. 'There was some talk of quarantining them here. Darwin might send staff.'

'I suppose it will depend on the medical treatment they need,' she said. She accepted his help down into the boat, then waited while he and Bill disposed of the extra stretchers they had carried.

The trip around the coast took an hour, and when she arrived she could see why Jack had radioed for extra help.

A canvas awning had been slung between trees and a makeshift hospital set up.

'Seems they ran out of food nearly a week ago, and what water they had was so rank I'm surprised it didn't kill them,' Jack told her. 'Some of these women and children are too weak to move until we've rehydrated them and, even then, we'll need stretchers. The Army is sending a helicopter to airlift the worst of them out and take them straight to Darwin, and the government is sending officers to man the hospital here.'

'So, where do I start?' Leonie asked.

'I'm checking the men now,' he said. 'Would you follow Jenny up the line of women and children? She's doing fluids, but if you could dress the worst of the festering sores and tropical ulcers they've developed. Once they're comfortable I'd like them classified into a four-tiered triage system, and coloured tags attached.'

Leonie understood. It was the usual procedure in situations where many patients were involved. She found the dressings and medication she would need and crossed to the first patient.

It was fourteen hours before she returned home, grateful to find an empty house. The car she'd taken to be Craig's was gone from the kerb.

She assumed that Deanne had returned and taken it, but she was too sickened by her recent experience to give that pair much thought. Two children had died before they could be airlifted out, and the gaunt faces and swollen bellies of the others haunted her exhausted sleep.

* * *

She woke at nine and phoned Susan at the Base, learning that her children had gone cheerfully off to school and that Jack was still on the island, treating the patients who had remained there.

'And what are your plans?' Susan asked.

'I think a spring-clean might be in order,' Leonie replied, although she couldn't explain that she wanted to rid the house of unpleasant memories and keep physically active so that she didn't think of the eventual fate of the boat people.

'Well, you won't feel like cooking after that kind of a day so come to dinner. I've already told your children to come back to my place because we weren't certain when you'd be back.'

Leonie agreed, warmed by the kind of friendship within their Base 'family' that surmounted all barriers.

She began in the living-room, worked through the kitchen and bathrooms, glanced at the children's rooms, deciding that she wasn't *that* energetic, then tackled her own bedroom.

Having stripped the sheets and washed them earlier, she let the bed air, pulling it away from the wall so that she could vacuum behind and beneath it.

A piece of paper caught in the nozzle of the vacuum cleaner, and she had to turn the machine off to free it. She smoothed it out, peering at the grainy reproduction in utter astonishment. It was a picture—barely discernible—of herself and Alex at the races in Talgoola. She had her arms around him and he held her tightly.

She tried to think but her brain had dissolved into blankness. She sank down on to the bed, her hands trembling as she tried to recall the moment. It must have been when number four had won and she'd turned to him to share her excitement. But she couldn't remember a photographer, a flash.

She looked again. The grainy texture blotted out all expression, but anyone seeing it would naturally assume that they were together. What was it doing down there at the end of the bed?

She rose swiftly, and pulled the bed further out. What else might be hidden there?

A newspaper article!

Her fingers were shaking so much that she could hardly spread it enough to make it legible. At the top was a photo of Alex and beneath an article on his multi-million-dollar company. The writer reported on his presence in Australia, mentioned his son's brush with death, Alex's generous donation to the FRDS and then went on to discuss the work he hoped to do at Coorawalla.

She put the two pages together and knew there was enough detail to recognise Alex in the second photo. She turned it over and read the name of a television channel. There was always television coverage of the Picnic Races—she'd seen the cameras there herself. And they'd have flown their footage out before the dust came down and isolated the town. It would have been on the television news on that Saturday night.

And Craig had recognised her! Once he'd had a photo taken from the television coverage and had found the article on Alex the rest would have been easy. Her name was listed in the Rainbow Bay telephone directory. She'd never changed it for fear of upsetting Mitchell!

Her stomach surged unpleasantly. It explained *how* Craig had found her, but not *why*!

Or did it? Once he had juxtaposed her into Alex's arms his greedy mind had smelt an opportunity to make some money! She wasn't certain how he meant to go about it but he would use the children, she knew that, and use his knowledge of her, his certainty that she would do anything to protect her children—even from the unsavoury knowledge that their father was a thief and a cheat.

She lay back on the unmade bed, trying to think the way Craig thought—trying to pre-empt whatever plan had been put on hold while he lay in that hospital bed.

Marrying Alex was the answer—marry him and take the children far beyond their father's reach.

But she'd run away once, and now knew that wouldn't work. And marrying Alex was the problem, not the solution. That was why Craig had come back. He hoped to milk Alex's money through her in some way.

So, don't marry Alex! her common sense declared. Solves a lot of problems if you forget that silly idea.

Tears gathered at the corners of her eyes and slid across her temples to dampen her hair.

You were happy before, she reminded herself. You've made a good life here for yourself and your kids.

It was the answer, but she lay and cried for what might have been before she decided that she'd wallowed in self-pity for long enough and got briskly off the bed, made it up with fresh sheets, and took herself into the shower to wash away the past. Then she phoned Coorawalla and spoke to Alex.

'So, when's the big announcement?' Susan asked, and six expectant faces turned her way.

'There's no big announcement!' she told them, a

cheerful smile hiding her shattered heart. 'I'm very fond of Alex, but I love my life here at the Bay.' Make it convincing, her head warned. 'Maybe I've been single too long to think about remarrying.'

'Oh, Mum, you seemed so happy with him!' Caroline cried.

'Well, I was but I'm sure he'll visit from time to time.' That was a lie! Alex had been adamant that he didn't want to be her 'friend'!

Eddie must have sensed her agony for he interrupted with news of the patients at Herd Island, and the talk became more general as the boys debated how they would manage to navigate the waters of the north.

She took Mitchell and Caroline home early, claiming tiredness after two exhausting days. Caroline wanted to talk about her decision, arguing that it was time Leonie had a life of her own. The daughter telling the mother! Leonie thought, but she repeated that she'd made up her mind.

Mitchell gave her a strange look and retreated to his bedroom. She hoped he'd get the message to his father, and Craig would head back to Melbourne as soon as he was released from hospital.

She slept badly again, waking to a dreary realisation that this was to be her life. Alex had opened a curtain and shown her glimpses of unexpected delights, and had left her aching for his touch.

It will pass, she told herself. You loved Craig once, and that pain passed.

Alex phoned again but she repeated her decision. Her mother phoned to tell her that she'd acted hastily and Caroline hovered over her as if she was an invalid, but

Leonie refused all offers of comfort, all words or advice.

The days passed, and the ache became such a familiar part of her that it was like a silent companion. She worked in the house or garden during the day—anything to tire her body so that sleep would be possible at night. After dinner she sat in the living-room, staring blindly at unremembered shows on the television. She was sitting there one evening when Mitchell, who'd been out to dinner with friends, burst in.

'I want to talk to you,' he announced, drawing up a chair opposite her and taking her hand in his. 'I want you to tell me about my father—all about him.'

She lifted her eyes and looked into his face, seeing a difference there that she couldn't understand. Was it maturity? Had he grown up while she was mourning?

'What kind of things?' she asked listlessly.

'Why you left him, for a start.' He sounded eager, which confused her.

'He left me first, Mitch,' she replied. 'Left me so often that I got tired of taking him back.'

'But there was more than that,' he insisted. 'Gran told me that, but said she wouldn't tell—she'd promised you.'

'He loved you, Mitch, and you loved him. Isn't that enough for you to know?'

'No, Mum, I want to know it all. I'm not a kid any more—I don't need to be protected.'

She almost smiled at that, but thought for a moment. Perhaps he should know! Perhaps being forewarned would protect him in the future.

'My father was in partnership with his brothers. We weren't wealthy in the way Alex is wealthy—' saying his name darted pain into her heart '—but we were well off.

Craig, I think, assumed we were better off than we were. He courted me, and I fell madly in love with him. We married, and my father found him a job in the business.

'I was never the right person for him,' she admitted. 'I realise that now! I was shy—too quiet—not flamboyant enough, but he thought I had money—or expectations of it—and that kept him coming back.'

'He left you straight away? As soon as you were married?' Mitchell's dreams of love were shattering before his youthful eyes.

'I don't think he ever gave up his old girlfriend,' she said sadly. 'And when she left there would be another one. He came back twice, repentant and contrite, and both times I got pregnant.'

She summoned up the strength to smile.

'You and Caroline are so dear to me that I could never regret my marriage,' she assured him, squeezing the hands that held hers.

'But my father?' Mitchell prompted.

Leonie shook her head.

'My father died and Craig expected I'd inherit money but my father's money was in the business and his share was willed so it stayed there, with Gran getting a regular annuity. Craig was furious! I'd never seen him so angry! He felt he'd been cheated—that I'd lied to him and defrauded him out of his expectations.'

She shook with horror as she remembered the scene, but now that the story was half-told she knew she had to finish it.

'So he took what he considered his!' she said baldly. 'He robbed the business of one hundred thousand dollars.

My uncles discovered it, and wanted to prosecute him. They said he'd never learn, otherwise.'

She looked at her son, remembering the little boy who'd cried and cried because they'd moved away and his father wouldn't be able to find them when he came back.

'You loved him, Mitch! I couldn't let him go to jail—to have you and Caroline grow up with that knowledge hanging over your heads. Gran sold her house and repaid the money, and we bribed your father to stay away from us for ever. Gran gave him another hundred thousand, and I left him with the house. I suppose he stayed away because he knew we had nothing left to give.'

'How did you set up again up here?' Mitchell wanted to know.

'Gran had enough to buy her cottage and my uncles loaned me money to buy this house. Gran minded you and I finished my nursing training and began work!'

She smiled into his pale face.

'We've managed OK, haven't we, Mitch?'

Did he know how much she wanted his understanding—his approval—for what she'd done?

'We've managed just fine, Mum,' he said, and she could see the mist of adolescent tears in his eyes.

'Well, Caro and I have,' he added. 'We couldn't have had a better upbringing. But isn't it time you started thinking of yourself? We're nearly off your hands. Why turn down Alex? Why not even talk it through with us—with him?'

Shock jolted through her. This was the last place she'd expected this conversation to lead.

'Is this the same young man who pointed out only weeks ago that I had you and Caroline and Gran so what more could I want? I think you also mentioned that he'd probably want someone younger and better-looking!'

'I was being selfish—and stupid!' he admitted. 'What's more, I won't be at home much longer, and who's going to look after you? Alex is a great guy.'

'It's impossible, Mitchell,' she said quietly, hearing her heart shatter into even smaller pieces. 'Impossible!'

'Because you don't love him?' this newly grown-up son persisted.

'Oh, no, I love him!' she murmured, and fancied she felt the air stir, as if Alex's ghost was in the house.

'Are you afraid of another marriage because your first one went so bad?'

She shook her head, wanting to stop him talking but knowing that they might never be this close again.

'Then it's because of Dad!' he said triumphantly. 'I knew it!'

His strange excitement startled her out of her welter of misery. After all she'd told him, he couldn't believe. . .!

'It is not because I still love your father, Mitchell! There can be no happy ending there. The man's married, for heaven's sake. I haven't thought about him, except occasionally with great relief that I'd left, for years and years and years.'

'I don't mean that!' he said impatiently. 'Even I could see he was a con-man! But he's got some hold over you. You've sent Alex away because you're frightened Dad will do something.'

She stared into his eyes, seeing her own, and tears began to slip down her cheeks. Reaching into her pocket, she brought out the two pieces of paper she'd carried like a bad omen for days. Smoothing them out, she handed them to him.

'I found them down behind my bed! Your father must have brought them up. It's why he came. Don't you see, Mitchell? All those years that he knew I had no money he left us alone, then suddenly he sees me on the television, apparently in Alex's arms, puts two and two together and heads back into our lives.'

'But how could he affect you and Alex?' Mitchell demanded. 'How could he hurt you once you'd remarried?'

Leonie shrugged.

'I don't know, Mitch, but I do know that's why he came. And he knows that I'll always be vulnerable through you and Caroline. He's a schemer, and he had some scheme to get through you to me and then to Alex's money.' She shrugged again. 'So the rest was easy. If I don't marry Alex there's no point in Craig's schemes. You and Caroline will be safe, and Alex will find someone else.'

'And you, my foolish, stupid, over-protective woman?'

Now Alex's ghost was talking and Mitchell was saying, 'See, I told you, Alex. It had to be my nuisance of a father who was causing the problem.'

Then she was in Alex's arms while he continued to scold her, punctuating his words with gentle kisses on her hair, her cheeks, her temples—wherever his lips would reach!

'Foolish woman,' he murmured. 'Did you not know I would sort out this problem—that I would protect your children as if they were my own?'

'But it isn't physical protection,' she argued agitatedly. If only it didn't feel so good to be in his arms! 'It's a more subtle blackmail that Craig would use. I've kept the past a secret all these years because I didn't want Mitchell and Caroline to think badly of their father. For all his weakness, he *is* their father. And he knew me well enough to know I wouldn't blacken his name to them. Even now, he would only need to come to Mitchell, pleading desperate trouble of some kind, and Mitchell would feel obliged to help.'

She saw Mitchell nod.

'So Mitchell could turn to me, and together we could work something out!' Alex suggested, and Leonie pushed away from him.

'No!' she cried vehemently. 'Can't you see, that's exactly what I feared would happen? Craig Cooper took my pride and self-respect, he took my uncles' money and my mother's generosity. I won't have him bleeding you, Alex. I won't have his shadow haunting my life. I won't cringe with shame every time I think you might be doling out money to that worthless con-artist. No marriage could survive that! You'd grow to hate me as much as I would hate myself. . .'

Alex stopped her tirade with a finger on her lips.

'I would not give in to blackmail!' he said severely. 'But Mitchell and I have successfully planned and carried out this little mission. He called me because you were so unhappy and we worked out what to do. I'm certain, between us, we can find a way to deal with your importunate ex-husband.'

He took her in his arms again, and looked down into her eyes.

'Have you so little faith in me?' he murmured.

She had no time to reply for his mouth had seized hers,

wiping out not only breath but thought as their tongues entwined and their bodies began to clamour for the ease they knew they could share.

'Besides,' Mitchell declared, carrying on the conversation as if his mother wasn't being passionately kissed in front of him, 'I've been talking to Alex about universities in Europe. He said he'd have me coached in Italian if I wanted to go to the medical school in Rome where he trained. Carlos is already there so it might be kind of fun!'

Even in its overwrought state, her mind assimilated the words and she pulled away from Alex.

'And have you sorted out Caroline's future as well?' she demanded, looking from her son to her lover.

'Oh, she's looking forward to going to school in Switzerland, and Eddie Stone says he'll send the twins over to visit us for their long vacations so we won't lose touch.'

'So?'

Alex's deep voice teased its way into her mind, and her demons danced so wildly that she felt as if she were being lifted into the air.

'Wings away, then?' Mitchell asked. 'I've explained to Alex I'll have to finish out the year at school, but then we can be off.'

His eyebrows lifted, as did Alex's. They were both waiting for a reply.

'Wings away!' she said, and slipped into two pairs of waiting arms.

MILLS & BOON®

AUGUST 1997 HARDBACK TITLES

ROMANCE

Haunted Spouse *Heather Allison*	H4692	0 263 15415 7
Satisfaction Guaranteed *Helen Brooks*	H4693	0 263 15416 5
Indiscretions *Robyn Donald*	H4694	0 263 15417 3
Scandalous Bride *Diana Hamilton*	H4695	0 263 15418 1
Outback Bride *Jessica Hart*	H4696	0 263 15419 X
Breakfast in Bed *Ruth Jean Dale*	H4697	0 263 15420 3
The Perfect Seduction *Penny Jordan*	H4698	0 263 15421 1
A Nanny Named Nick *Miranda Lee*	H4699	0 263 15422 X
Fletcher's Baby! *Anne McAllister*	H4700	0 263 15423 8
Rent-A-Cowboy *Barbara McMahon*	H4701	0 263 15424 6
The Only Solution *Leigh Michaels*	H4702	0 263 15425 4
Love Can Wait *Betty Neels*	H4703	0 263 15426 2
To Marry a Stranger *Renee Roszel*	H4704	0 263 15427 0
The Youngest Sister *Anne Weale*	H4705	0 263 15428 9
Willing to Wed *Cathy Williams*	H4706	0 263 15429 7
The Vengeful Groom *Sara Wood*	H4707	0 263 15430 0

HISTORICAL ROMANCE™

An Illustrious Lord *Helen Dickson*	H413	0 263 15441 6
The Unconventional Miss Dane *Francesca Shaw*	H414	0 263 15442 4

MEDICAL ROMANCE™

A Heart of Gold *Jessica Matthews*	M331	0 263 15439 4
Wings of Love *Meredith Webber*	M332	0 263 15440 8

MILLS & BOON®

AUGUST 1997 LARGE PRINT TITLES

ROMANCE

Mistaken for a Mistress *Jacqueline Baird*	1023	0 263 15165 4
Lovers' Lies *Daphne Clair*	1024	0 263 15166 2
Runaway Honeymoon *Ruth Jean Dale*	1025	0 263 15167 0
Night of Shame *Miranda Lee*	1026	0 263 15168 9
The Daughter of the Manor *Betty Neels*	1027	0 263 15169 7
Looking After Dad *Elizabeth Oldfield*	1028	0 263 15170 0
A Business Engagement *Jessica Steele*	1029	0 263 15171 9
The Guilty Wife *Sally Wentworth*	1030	0 263 15172 7

HISTORICAL ROMANCE™

Madselin's Choice *Elizabeth Henshall*	0 263 15181 6
Lady Clairval's Marriage *Paula Marshall*	0 263 15182 4

MEDICAL ROMANCE™

If You Need Me... *Caroline Anderson*	0 263 15097 6
A Surgeon to Trust *Janet Ferguson*	0 263 15098 4
Valentine's Husband *Josie Metcalfe*	0 263 15099 2
Wings of Passion *Meredith Webber*	0 263 15100 X

TEMPTATION®

Angel Baby *Leandra Logan*	0 263 15461 0
The Drifter *Vicki Lewis Thompson*	0 263 15462 9

MILLS & BOON®

SEPTEMBER 1997 HARDBACK TITLES

ROMANCE

Do You Take This Cowboy? *Jeanne Allan*	H4708	0 263 15471 8
A Fragile Marriage *Rosalie Ash*	H4709	0 263 15472 6
Reckless Engagement *Daphne Clair*	H4710	0 263 15473 4
The Courting Campaign *Catherine George*	H4711	0 263 15474 2
Baby in the Boardroom *Rosemary Gibson*	H4712	0 263 15475 0
Perfect Marriage Material *Penny Jordan*	H4713	0 263 15476 9
Lovestruck *Charlotte Lamb*	H4714	0 263 15477 7
Temporary Husband *Day Leclaire*	H4715	0 263 15478 5
Rainy Day Kisses *Debbie Macomber*	H4716	0 263 15479 3
A Marriage to Remember *Carole Mortimer*	H4717	0 263 15480 7
Kissed by a Stranger *Valerie Parv*	H4718	0 263 15481 5
Christmas with a Stranger *Catherine Spencer*	H4719	0 263 15482 3
The Groom's Revenge *Kate Walker*	H4720	0 263 15483 1
Expectations *Shannon Waverly*	H4721	0 263 15484 X
A Very Public Affair *Sally Wentworth*	H4722	0 263 15485 8
No Wife Required! *Rebecca Winters*	H4723	0 263 15486 6

HISTORICAL ROMANCE™

The Ruby Pendant *Mary Nichols*	H415	0 263 15446 7
Letters to a Lady *Gail Whitiker*	H416	0 263 15495 5

MEDICAL ROMANCE™

Wait and See *Sharon Kendrick*	M333	0 263 15443 2
Too Close for Comfort *Jessica Matthews*	M334	0 263 15444 0

MILLS & BOON®

SEPTEMBER 1997 LARGE PRINT TITLES

ROMANCE

Craving Jamie *Emma Darcy*	1031	0 263 15199 9
The Second Bride *Catherine George*	1032	0 263 15203 0
His Brother's Child *Lucy Gordon*	1033	0 263 15204 9
The Secret Wife *Lynne Graham*	1034	0 263 15208 1
Wedding Daze *Diana Hamilton*	1035	0 263 15209 X
Kiss and Tell *Sharon Kendrick*	1036	0 263 15213 8
Finn's Twins! *Anne McAllister*	1037	0 263 15214 6
An Innocent Charade *Patricia Wilson*	1038	0 263 15218 9

HISTORICAL ROMANCE™

Miranda's Masquerade *Meg Alexander*	0 263 15239 1
Changing Fortunes *Polly Forrester*	0 263 15243 X

MEDICAL ROMANCE™

A Midwife's Challenge *Frances Crowne*	0 263 15141 7
Full Recovery *Lilian Darcy*	0 263 15142 5
Doctor Across the Lagoon *Margaret Holt*	0 263 15143 3
Lakeland Nurse *Gill Sanderson*	0 263 15144 1

TEMPTATION®

Look into my Eyes *Glenda Sanders*	0 263 15463 7
The Lawman *Vicki Lewis Thompson*	0 263 15464 5